MW00721476

Root Causes

Root Causes

With my best wishes

Elaine

Elaine Kozak

IGUANA

Copyright © 2014 Elaine Kozak
Published by Iguana Books
720 Bathurst Street, Suite 303
Toronto, Ontario, Canada
M5V 2R4

All rights reserved. No part of this publication may be reproduced, stored in a
retrieval system or transmitted, in any form or by any means, electronic, mechanical,
recording or otherwise (except brief passages for purposes of review) without the
prior permission of the author or a licence from The Canadian Copyright Licensing
Agency (Access Copyright). For an Access Copyright licence, visit
www.accesscopyright.ca or call toll free to 1-800-893-5777.

Publisher: Greg Ioannou
Editor: Andrea Douglas
Front cover image: Mark Teasdale
Author photo: Evan Gateho
Front cover design: Meghan Behse
Book layout design: Meghan Behse

Library and Archives Canada Cataloguing in Publication

Kozak, Elaine Louise, 1950-, author
        Root causes / Elaine Kozak.

Issued in print and electronic formats.
ISBN 978-1-77180-032-7 (pbk.).--ISBN 978-1-77180-033-4 (epub).--
ISBN 978-1-77180-034-1 (mobi).--ISBN 978-1-77180-035-8 (pdf)

        I. Title.

PS8621.O9783R66 2014   C813'.6   C2013-908524-6
                                            C2013-908525-4

This is the original print edition of *Root Causes*.

In memory of my father, Michael Kozak

Poet, musician, farmer

and

For Marcel

Chapter 1

When Melanie told me Leo was dead, my first thought was, *Well, that's that.* She was crying, and I felt a moment's irritation at her tears; she had never really liked him. I must have dozed off, because the next thing I knew it was night and I was alone and the knowledge of Leo's death sat like a malevolent cat on my chest, sucking the breath from my mouth. There was a strong smell of bleach in the ward, and a whiff of it still evokes that sense of crushing sadness. I could write a book about the many and varied dimensions of misery I passed through stuck in that hospital bed; this isn't it. But this story begins with Leo.

I've often thought about my initial reaction to Leo's death. Was my brain still scrambled from my head injury? Was I numbed out on painkillers? Or, in that moment of unguarded thought, was I simply accepting what I had always feared, that our improbable union couldn't last?

I couldn't say what had drawn Leo to me. In age, he was almost ten years older; in maturity, probably more. He was all cutting-edge art, vintage cars, cult wines. I ... well, I hadn't done much more in my life than finish my MBA and grind away in the belly of a big multinational accounting firm. My wardrobe ran to five suits in neutral colours, one for each day of the week, and a drawer full of white blouses. I had no expectations of romance. I learned early on that most men saw tall, plain women like me as losers who are grateful for any attention they get, and the only relationships I had were of the episodic, tumble-into-bed-and-go-your-own-way-in-the-morning kind. Which suited me fine. My main goal in life was to achieve financial independence.

Leo was different. He was one of the senior managers at a natural gas company where my boss Simon, a colleague Jim, and I had undertaken an operational audit. When we had presented our findings to the executive committee, I had noticed Leo because he was taller than anyone else in the room and completely bald. Two weeks later I was queuing for my lunch at a sushi stall in a food court near my office when a voice behind me said, "Hello, Clare, isn't it?" I remembered Leo, but not his name, jumbled as it was among those of his colleagues.

"Leonardo Barsoni," he said, extending his hand. "Everyone calls me Leo."

When I shook his hand it seemed like all of me was caught in the grip of his cool, dry fingers. I could feel the pressure of the signet ring he wore and the grain of his skin, not rough but textured. "Next!" the server at the counter said, and, somewhat dazed, I withdrew my hand from Leo's, requested my food, and shifted down the line to wait for it. Leo placed his own order and followed.

"Are you meeting anyone?" he said.

I had planned to return to my desk and eat with one hand while editing a report with the other. "No," I said.

The server handed our food over the counter and invited us to help ourselves to chopsticks and soy sauce. Leo accepted his plastic clamshell of sushi and said, "Then would you mind if I joined you?"

When we had found and sat down at a table, Leo spoke, but I was contemplating my wooden chopsticks, wondering if it would be rude to rub them together as I usually did to smooth out the rough edges, and missed what he said.

"Sorry?" I said, my face reddening.

Leo smiled at me, a slow, generous smile. I stared at him like a deer caught in headlights. Somehow I got through the meal and in my rush to leave found myself accepting an invitation to dinner.

Over the next few months, we went out from time to time, usually dinner, but also to concerts, gallery openings, wine tastings, and even, once, a political debate. I wondered at Leo's lack of sexual interest in me, but wasn't surprised. I'm not what most men would consider *hot,* and who knew, maybe his inclinations lay elsewhere. But Leo was such good company that it didn't matter. Then he invited me to come home with him one night, and after that I spent more and more time at his place until it became every weekend when he wasn't away on his frequent trips. After almost three years, he suggested I move in.

Somewhere along the way I fell in love with Leo, but it was so gradual that I didn't mark the occasion. Or maybe it happened when we first shook hands and I didn't know it.

***

The crash happened in mid-December 1998 on the Stanley Park Causeway when we were on our way to West Vancouver for a Christmas party at the home of Leo's boss. It had been raining, and Leo's 1965 Porsche 911 somehow spun around and was T-boned by the car behind us. Leo had loved that car, restoring different parts as they wore out over the years, but it had only lap seat belts and no airbags.

I saw pictures of what was left of the Porsche. The driver's door had been ripped off and the frame pancaked into the car's centre. A starburst of cracks on the passenger window marked the spot where my head had connected. Leo took the brunt of the impact; I only hope he died quickly.

Among all that I lost that night was my favourite dress. The emergency room staff cut it off when they prepped me for surgery. I got the dress while Leo and I were in San Francisco one weekend. He said he didn't mind accompanying me while I shopped and hummed noncommittally when I showed him the practical little black dresses I planned to try on. There was a knock on the door while I was in the change room, and when I opened it the saleslady thrust a clothes hanger through the crack. On the hanger hung, with more life than I've seen in some people, a sleek sheath made of midnight blue silk whose folds caught and tossed back the feeble light. It slid over my shoulders with a soft hiss and settled on my body as if it had come home. The top cut away sharply from the shoulders to form a deep décolletage, and my hand automatically rose to my neck to cover the expanse of skin left exposed. The waist nipped in, and the skirt hugged my thighs. I stepped out of the change room and smiled uncertainly at Leo.

"What do you think?"

"Nice," he said.

I returned to the cubicle and slowly peeled the dress off. There was no price tag, and I debated whether to bother asking. I was pretty sure it cost more than I could afford, but I knew I had to have it. When I handed the dress over to the saleslady and started to pull out my wallet, she gave me a conspiratorial smile and told me it had been taken care of. She folded the dress carefully in several layers of tissue and slid it into a bag that was sitting at the ready. Back at our hotel, I found that the bag also contained some filmy briefs and a bra whose frothy lace hid its cunning engineering. It collected my breasts like errant apples, held them up like offerings, and suddenly I had cleavage.

I had put the dress on and was admiring myself in the angled mirror that stood in a corner of our bedroom when Leo came home that awful night. He was running late and immediately started dressing for the evening. Apart from a brief greeting, he didn't say anything. I hadn't lived with him long enough to know all his moods, so I let him be and started to twist my hair into a French knot. I had grown it long and wore it up at Leo's suggestion. One night, a few months after I had met him, he had leaned across the dinner table and brushed my heavy fringe off my forehead.

"Why do you cover your face?" he said.

I pulled away and laughed awkwardly. I take after my Estonian father, the same long bony face, ash brown hair, and eyes that are sometimes blue and sometimes green. I also inherited his height and long limbs.

"Concealment," I said. "I'm not exactly pretty."

"Not pretty, no," Leo agreed. "Your features are too strong. Handsome, rather."

"Handsome?"

"Yes. Your eyes, especially, are very fine."

Even now those eyes, so fine, tear up remembering that singularly rare praise.

I secured the knot with one last hairpin and reached for a sapphire pendant Leo had given me on my birthday. "You're awfully quiet tonight. Rather not go?" I said, glancing over my shoulder.

"It's not an option." Leo fished around in the little wooden box inlaid with ebony that sat on top of his armoire, found the cufflinks he wanted, and poked them into place. "I'm just a bit tired. I'm going to make a cup of coffee. Do you want one?"

I shook my head.

He picked up his jacket from the bed. "Clare … we need to talk." His voice was different than usual, flat, dull.

"Is something wrong?"

"No." He hesitated. "Not really. Something's come up. Something from a very long time ago." He slipped his arm around my waist and kissed my neck. "We'll talk tomorrow," he said, releasing me.

It's the last thing I remember.

Chapter 2

I spent twelve days in hospital. My mother stayed at my side until the surgeon declared me out of danger. She sat for hours on a hard metal chair by my bed, occasionally touching my battered face, her fingertips like moths. My father came in between trips home to shower and shave and to the college where he taught music. He seemed badly shaken by my brush with death and spent his time staring with reddened eyes out the window in my room, whistling shreds of melodies under his breath. Melanie slipped in and out whenever her two young sons and her work let her. As pretty as I was plain, she had landed a job right out of college with a local television network and enjoyed a certain celebrity in the city thanks to her role hosting a hip lifestyle show.

I had only two other visitors.

One was Adrienne, the administrative assistant to my work unit. She reported with relish that my absence had disrupted the work schedule to the point that Simon, our boss, who she considered an overpaid slacker, had to cancel the Caribbean cruise he had booked for the new year.

The other visitor came twice.

The first time was shortly after I had come out of surgery and was swimming in and out of consciousness. Once when I opened my eyes, a dark shape filled my field of vision. It bent forward, and a man spoke, his breath minty and warm against my face.

"Are you awake?" he said.

I held his gaze to keep from slipping back into sleep and pursed my lips to ask who he was, but all that came out was a puff of air.

"She is in no condition to speak to you. I think you should leave," my mother said. Her Scottish brogue was thick over the words, as it had been whenever she had scolded us.

"I'll come back when you're better," the man said softly, and left.

A few days later I lay in my bed, disgruntled after an argument with my doctor on one of his morning rounds. "I'm fine," I had declared. "Why can't I go home?"

The doctor glanced at me from under his brows as he scribbled something on my chart. "You've had a serious head injury and surgery," he said. "Things seem to be coming along fine, but I think we need to keep an eye on you for a few more days."

"Yes, but what am I supposed to *do*?" I said to the doctor's departing back. The bandage that encased my head covered one of my eyes, making it difficult to read the books and magazines my family had brought, and I was tired of the television's mindless chatter and maudlin holiday programming.

"You seem much better," an unknown but not unfamiliar voice said. I focused my good eye on the speaker, a young man of Chinese descent who was pulling the metal chair up to the side of my bed. He sat down and leaned forward, forearms resting on thighs, hands clasped.

"You were here once before."

The man nodded. "I wanted to talk to you, but I guess it was too soon."

"Who are you?"

"I am Inspector Yuen from the city police." He extended a hand, and I grasped it sideways, adjusting his age up a few years. "I want to ask you about the car crash."

"The crash? Okay."

"Can you tell me how it happened?"

"No, I don't remember anything."

"Nothing at all?"

"I remember being at home, dressing to go, but I don't even recall leaving. The next thing was waking up here."

"That's it?"

I nodded.

The inspector was silent for a moment. "I've got a bit of a problem. The crash wasn't an accident."

I levered myself up higher against the pillows with my elbows. "What do you mean? What else could it have been?"

"There was this other car. According to witnesses, it kept ramming into the back of yours until, I guess, yours spun out of control, and then it hit you broadside."

"Why on earth would anyone do that?"

"That's what I'm trying to find out."

"Why don't you ask whoever was driving that car?"

"The car was abandoned in North Vancouver. It had been stolen. The owner was out of town the night the crash happened, so we don't know who was driving it."

"Was it maybe some kids joyriding? Not able to handle the car?"

"Maybe. But if it was kids, they'd have smartened up after the first time they hit you. You were rammed several times in what sounds like a pretty deliberate manner. I think something was going on; someone had an issue with one of you. Tell me, were you or your friend maybe in some kind of trouble? Were either of you having problems with anyone?"

I frowned, and the bandage pinched my forehead. "No."

"Think again. Any reason why someone might want to hurt either of you? Old boyfriends? Girlfriends? Husbands or wives who were cheated on?"

"No, no. There was nothing like that."

"Disagreements at work? Business debts? Or maybe some disputes over drugs?"

"No, of course not!" I eased back against the pillows but held Inspector Yuen's gaze. He studied me for a few moments, rubbing his chin.

"How long had you known Leo?"

"A few years."

"How well did you know him?"

How well do you know anyone? I thought. "Well enough, I guess."

"Was he involved in anything, well, dubious?

"Leo? No, absolutely not."

"Any unusual behaviour? Like, did he go off and do things that he wouldn't tell you about, or have telephone calls he kept secret? Or were there any unexplained absences?"

"None that I knew of. He had work commitments, certainly, and he travelled a lot with his job, but nothing I'd call 'unexplained.'"

"How about his family, his friends? Any you wondered about?"

"He didn't have any family and not that many friends." It suddenly struck me how solitary Leo had been. I hadn't minded not having to share him with anyone else. "Just some of the guys he worked with."

"Anything out of the ordinary happen recently?"

With each question, Inspector Yuen had leaned in closer to me, to the point that I could see a small, white scar on his cheekbone and smell the musk of his aftershave. His voice was soft and seductive, and I felt a compelling urge to provide an answer, *any* answer, to make him happy. Then I remembered something my father had told me once, a caution born of his uncertain childhood in Soviet Estonia.

I had been fourteen, and we had been driving—rushing, really—to the hospital, where Melanie had just been admitted with a ruptured appendix. The police pulled us over, and when the officer questioned Dad he admitted to exceeding the speed limit and meekly accepted the ticket given to him.

9

"Why didn't you tell him that we were on our way to the hospital because of a medical emergency?" I'd asked. "Maybe he wouldn't have written the ticket."

My father had glanced at me. "Never give authorities more information than necessary," he said.

"There's been nothing out of the ordinary recently," I said to the inspector. "Look, does it really matter now? It's done. Leo's dead." My voice caught on the last words.

Inspector Yuen snapped back in his chair. "Leo was *killed,* and you were badly hurt. At the least it was a case of hit and run. Don't you want whoever did this to you to be caught?"

"I suppose. I can't believe, though, that someone was after us. Maybe it was a case of random road rage."

"Maybe." Yuen's tone implied that he seriously doubted it. He continued to probe insistently, but I shrugged and shook my head with regret. Eventually he concluded that he wasn't going to get anything more out of me. "Be sure to let me know if you think of anything or remember more about that night," he said as he stood up to go.

"Of course," I said.

After Inspector Yuen left, I puzzled over what he had told me. Could someone really have been after us? I could think of nothing in my uneventful life that had gained me any enemies. And Leo? He was the kind of guy who didn't drink and drive, paid his taxes, dropped coins into the caps of beggars. It was hard to believe that anyone would have a problem with him. *No,* I concluded, *the crash was just one of those inexplicable karmic events that mess up our lives.*

Chapter 3

Our parents had recently downsized from the family home to a condo with limited guest accommodations, so when it was time to leave I accepted Melanie's invitation to stay with her in the large house she and her husband, Dave, owned in one of the upscale parts of town. As Melanie helped me dress in the street clothes she had collected from Leo's condo, she lightly touched the shaved part of my skull. The scar from the surgery was still hot and livid, but my head felt cool and impossibly light without the bandage. "You need something to put on your head. I never thought of that." She looked around the curtained-off cubicle that separated my bed from the other one in the room. "Hang on. I think there's a toque in the back of the car. I'll run down and get it."

I listlessly transferred the books and magazines, skin cream, lozenges, and other articles that had accumulated in the drawers of my side table into the small leather grip Melanie had brought. I had hated my time in hospital, but at least it had held purpose: to leave. Now I couldn't see beyond the going.

Melanie returned with the toque, a navy tube made from synthetic yarn with the logo of a brake and muffler shop stitched on one side.

"Sorry, it's not that great, but it will get you to the car," she said. She tucked stray bits of my remaining hair under the toque and turned the edge up all the way around. "Not bad," she said, stepping back to survey the results. She picked up the bag, and we left.

***

The next morning I sat in Melanie's solarium breakfast nook nursing a weak cup of coffee and looking out the window. Hanging containers of seeds and suet on a couple of apple trees brought in a steady stream of birds to the yard: sparrows, robins, juncos, and a jay whose brilliant blue plumage lit up the grey day. The birds pecked and squabbled and flitted about, scattering in feathered frenzy when Melanie's marmalade tom, Christopher, crept into view. The birds had attracted other cats besides Christopher: a pretty tortoiseshell with a harlequin face who flirted shamelessly with him, running her feathery tail under his nose, and a big, black jaguar-like beast that lay under the rhododendron bush and kept watch with topaz eyes.

Melanie sat down at the table with a sigh and poured a cup of tea from a pot she had made before feeding the boys. She tasted the tea, made a face, and pushed the cup away. "Clare, sweetie, you should eat something. You're positively skeletal."

I picked up the toast that had grown cold on my plate and nibbled on a corner. We had reverted to our traditional roles: Melanie, gently bossy; me, seemingly compliant. I caught a movement out of the corner of my eye. Christopher had spotted the black cat and was advancing upon him in a crouch.

"And we have to do something about your hair."

A sharp yowl emanated from the backyard, and a flash of orange and black twisted out of the frame.

"I'm fine," I said, turning to Melanie. "I doubt I'd be able to get an appointment this close to New Year's. I'll just keep the toque on."

"I think I mentioned that Dave and I've invited a bunch of people over tomorrow for New Year's." Melanie reached for the telephone. "I'll call Philip."

From what I heard of the conversation between Melanie and Philip, her stylist, he tried very hard to fob me off on one of his junior cutters. But Melanie was implacable, and it was to Philip's chair that I was shown later in the morning. He was not well pleased to have to fit me into his full day, but Melanie did her celebrity thing and thanked him prettily for the favour. Philip curled his mouth in a plastic smile and said that it was no problem, really. Melanie promised to be back in an hour to pick me up, and left.

Philip's smile vanished when he pulled the toque off my head. "Oh, my ..." He ran his hand lightly over my butchered scalp. "You poor dear. What happened?"

I explained briefly, and Philip studied my reflection in the mirror at his station. His scrutiny was discomfiting, and after a long moment he spoke.

"You know, the best, really, would be to shave all the rest off."

Leo had shaved his narrow tonsure every morning. Tears pricked my eyes.

"Yes, take it all off," I said. It would be a small act of homage.

"You're sure?" Philip said. "I don't want any meltdowns after."

"Yes, yes, just get it over with."

Philip smiled, a genuine one, whipped a black cape emblazoned with his salon's name over my front, and fastened it at the back. "You may really like it. Some women do it regularly. Very bold." He picked up his razor and fiddled with the setting. "A number one cut, I think," he said, and set the device buzzing.

It didn't take long. When Philip was done he undid the cape and shook it out, and we studied my reflection in silence. *Tabula rasa*. The contours of my skull stood out in relief, and the surgery scar cut a ragged red line across the side of my head. My hollow cheeks, testament to weeks of shock and deprivation, exaggerated the angular lines of my face, and yellow bruise traces discoloured the skin around my eyes. I looked like a tortured saint in an El Greco painting. I thanked Philip, pulled on my toque, and left, hoping to score some decent java before Melanie returned.

***

Despite, or possibly because of, my new hairstyle, Melanie didn't protest much when I proposed to stay in my room rather than joining the party. I sat propped up against the pillows in my bed, trying to read, but the thump of the music playing downstairs was distracting. I finally set the book aside and gave myself over to melancholic thoughts about the new year.

The last one had started with such promise. Leo and I were concluding a week-long vacation in Cancun. New Year's Eve had been a magical night, the fulcrum between the old and the new year, between past and possibility. We spent the evening shuffling around to bossa nova rhythms, which was all the dance band at the resort seemed able to play. As midnight approached, we grabbed a bottle of champagne and a couple of glasses and abandoned the crowd. We walked to the boulders that demarcated one end of the resort's beach, our bare feet sinking into the cool, moist sand. We squeezed into an opening in the rocks that we had discovered previously. Over the boom and hiss of the surf, we heard the countdown to twelve o'clock start. Leo popped the cork and poured out the foaming wine. When a cheer signaled midnight's arrival, he kissed me, clinked my glass, and said, "To a great year."

It had been, until the car crash.

Now the future looked bleak. My life would revert to the dull plod it had been before I met Leo. I would no doubt have to move out of his condo. My own, an affordable but gloomy hole in the wall that overlooked a parking lot, was rented out with over a year remaining on the lease, so I would need to find another place to live until it was available. Both would be a step down from Leo's suite, with its airiness and views out to English Bay. Then there was the matter of work. I wasn't sure when I'd be well enough to return to my job, or how much sick pay I was entitled to. And, worst of all, I'd be all alone again.

How was it, I thought bitterly, that some people seemed to have it all, the pretty and the privileged, girls like Melanie, with their good looks, glittering careers, perfect marriages? And then there were the rest of us who never seemed to catch a break. I sniffled a bit, thinking about this, until I remembered something else my father had told me. I had been nine or ten and sobbing out some tale of schoolyard woe into his shirt front.

"No, it's not fair," he had said, stroking my hair, "but tears won't get you justice."

Oh well, I thought, blowing my nose, *I had always known that Leo was too good to be true.*

***

My strength returned slowly over the next ten days. I had an appointment with my doctor on the afternoon of the eleventh. Melanie had offered to give me a ride, and when I came down from my room I carried my few belongings in the leather grip.

"Are you sure you're ready to go?" Melanie said. "You know you're welcome to stay as long as you like."

I touched her lightly on the shoulder. "I'm fine, and it's time."

My blazer and loafers weren't adequate for the wet snow that was sheeting down, so Melanie lent me Dave's anorak and duck boots. Dave was about my height, and his rather dainty feet were only slighter larger than my own. I didn't need a hat; the toque had become a permanent fixture on my head.

After the appointment, during which the doctor proclaimed my recovery well on track, I called a cab and made the journey home. At the door of Leo's condo, I took a deep breath, turned the key, and stepped into deep gloom. The ineffable odour of disuse was slowly replaced by all the faint, familiar smells of my old life: leather, aftershave, books, coffee. I shook tears from my eyes and turned on the light. After shedding Dave's jacket and boots, I carried the grip to the bedroom. The shirt Leo had taken off when he had changed into evening clothes was thrown across the back of a chair, and a pair of his shoes was tucked under it, one lying on its side. Coins and keys from Leo's pocket and the electronic pass card to the elevator in his office tower sat in a little dish on the bureau.

I can't stay in here, I thought. I hauled down sheets, blankets, and pillows from the linen closet and carried them to the room that had served as Leo's den. I disgorged the foldaway bed from the blue tweed sofa that had accommodated his infrequent guests, dumped the bedding on the shallow mattress, and sat down on the edge. I considered returning to Melanie's; this was going to be harder than I had thought.

A flashing light on the telephone sitting on Leo's desk caught my attention. I wondered idly how long it had been blinking. I got up, picked up the receiver, and keyed in the code to access the voice mail. A tart voice informed me that the mailbox was full and I should promptly listen to and delete unwanted messages. A succession of clicks was interspersed with a couple of condolence calls and a message from a woman named Karen Meyers, who identified herself as Leo's lawyer and asked me to call her at my earliest convenience. The digital clock on the desk indicated that, despite the deepening dusk, the work day had not yet ended, so I dialed the lawyer's number.

When we had completed introductions, Karen Meyers informed me that she was the executor of Leo's will and that there were a number of matters to be dealt with and decisions to be made. She declined to elaborate on the telephone, and we arranged to meet at eleven o'clock the following morning.

I slept better than I had expected to and woke with only a trace of a headache. A quick check of the refrigerator the previous evening had released a miasma of sour and rotting food, so I showered and dressed quickly and went in search of breakfast before my appointment with Karen Meyers. Without thinking, I had put on Dave's anorak and duck boots. *You look like a bag lady,* I said to my reflection in the elevator mirror while riding up to Karen Meyer's office on the twentieth floor of one of the city's sleek glass towers. I tugged my toque lower on my forehead and stepped out of the elevator.

The legal firm Karen worked for occupied the entire floor. Karen's office was in a choice spot on the outside wall. When her secretary led me there, Karen rose from behind her desk and extended her hand. I gripped it briefly and she waved me to a chair. The floor-to-ceiling windows in the office would have commanded a view of the port if it hadn't been obscured by a dense fog. The effect was one of floating in the clouds. Karen had opted for a traditional look in her decor. Her desk and credenza were mahogany wood, as were the bookcases that lined one wall. The burgundy leather chair I sat down in was pocked with buttons, and its raised arms held my own up in the unnatural rounded posture of a hard plastic doll.

"So you're Clare," Karen said, a slight smile playing with her mouth.

I admitted as much, and we studied each other for a moment. There was a thick and fleshy quality to Karen, but her face was more than passably pretty and she was, as Melanie would say, well put together, from the pale, expertly cut and subtly frosted hair to the artfully applied makeup. A leopard pattern scarf at her throat matched her tawny eyes, and finely drawn arched brows had frozen her in an attitude of mild skepticism. I can only imagine what she made of me in my toque and anorak.

"A tragic accident."

"Yes," I said. I could hardly disagree.

"I made the necessary arrangements according to Leo's wishes," Karen said. She pushed a small card towards me. "This is where the ashes are."

The card was for a columbarium not far from the city centre. The number of the niche where Leo's ashes had been placed was written down on the bottom.

I stared at the card for a moment, then slipped it into my pocket. "Thanks." I shifted in my chair. "I'll get my stuff out of the condo as soon as I can. I'll need a week or so." I wasn't sure where I'd go. Maybe Melanie could put me up again until I found a place.

Karen eyed me quizzically. "You don't have to move. The condo is yours."

"Well, no. We didn't own it jointly. It's in Leo's name."

"I know, but Leo left it to you."

I straightened up in my chair. "He did?"

"Yes, and with the exception of a couple of charity bequests and a painting, everything else. Much of the other stuff is what you'd expect. In addition to the condo and chattels, you're the beneficiary of his life insurance policy, the survivor benefits associated with his company pension, and all of his savings and investments. These are held mostly with his bank." Karen mentioned the downtown branch of one of the large chartered banks.

I nodded but without completely grasping what it meant. *Why me?* I wondered. "I know that Leo didn't have any remaining family, but is there no one else?"

"Apparently not." Karen shifted some papers in the file before her. "Oh, yes, there's also the property on South Salish Island."

I frowned. "The property on South Salish Island? I'm sorry, I'm not familiar with it." I felt foolish admitting this and was grateful that Karen was busy studying the document and didn't seem to have noticed.

"Leo bought it last year." She looked up at me. "I was away then—my husband took his sabbatical in France—so another lawyer here dealt with it."

"What kind of a property is it?"

Karen turned a page over. "Hard to say. It's thirty-five acres. Probably intended as a vacation retreat. That's mostly what there is on those islands."

I had spent the last half of the previous year in Milwaukee working on a merger between a Canadian and a Milwaukee-based industrial controls company. It would make my career, Simon had said. Promotion was hinted at. After the first of six long months, I'd realized that I had been offered the project because no one else wanted it. I was away for three weeks of each month, then came home for the fourth. There would have been ample opportunity for Leo to buy the property without my knowing, but why would he not have told me?

"You mentioned a painting?" I said, changing the subject.

"Oh, yes." Karen pulled the papers in the file back into a pile and aligned the edges. "That's for me." She smiled at my surprise. "Leo wasn't just my client; we were close friends."

A small screw of jealously pierced my chest.

"Actually, we were an item once, when we were in university."

The screw tightened.

"But, of course, that was a very long time ago."

At least one husband and two kids ago, I thought, looking at the family photo that sat in a filigreed gold frame on the credenza behind her.

"We discovered that we were better off as friends than as, well, lovers."

"Ah," I said, and smiled to show that it didn't matter in the least to me.

"Leo said he would be my first client, and he was."

"I see. And the painting? Which one is it?" I mentally surveyed the art hanging in the condo. Some were by well-known artists and, from what I knew, worth a fair bit.

"A stormy seascape in gold and grey. It was the first of what Leo said would become his collection. I helped him pick it out."

I nodded. I had looked at the painting just that morning. It held pride of place over Leo's desk. Leaving it to Karen was a curiously intimate gesture. I wondered which of them had broken off their relationship. "Is that it?" I said. It sounded greedy so I quickly added, "I mean, what happens next?"

Karen closed the folder and smoothed it with her palms. "I'll begin probate. It's fairly straightforward, so it shouldn't take too long to complete. Do you have a lawyer with whom I should work?"

I didn't have a lawyer, and I really didn't want to start looking for one. "No, it's okay," I said airily. "You can just deal with me."

***

Apart from feeling relief at not having to move, I felt uncomfortable with my inheritance, undeserving of such consideration.

"Clare, you're being ridiculous," Melanie said when I tried to explain these feelings to her. She had come over to see how I was doing, and after seeing me camped out in the den, she had offered to clear the bedroom of Leo's things. "Most people in your position would be ecstatic. What's your problem?"

"I wasn't with Leo that long, and it just doesn't feel right. Then there's that South Salish property. I didn't even know about it." This bothered me the most. It wasn't a trivial purchase. Why had Leo not mentioned it, discussed his plans with me? Why had he kept it a secret?

Melanie folded the last shirt and placed it in a cardboard box. "Couples don't always share everything. Dave sure doesn't tell me all about his business stuff."

"I guess so."

Melanie zipped the flaps of the boxes shut with packing tape. She was going to take Leo's clothes to a charity on whose board she served, which, among other things, provided clothing to the dispossessed who were trying to find jobs. I entertained the surreal image of homeless men pushing their carts around Vancouver's skid row dressed in Leo's bespoke suits and Egyptian cotton shirts, and shook my head to clear it.

"Come on," she said, "look on the bright side. Think of all the things you can do now."

"Maybe," I said.

***

I left cleaning out Leo's desk to the end, a task I kept for myself. The seascape painting hung on the wall against which the desk sat, and I studied it briefly before starting. The panel was about three feet by four and edged with a discreet frame. An illegible signature scored the lower left-hand corner. The artist had avoided the banality that the subject typically inspired by infusing the brooding sky and turbulent waters with a crystalline luminosity. *Very nice,* I thought, *but not mine.* I took it off the wall and carried it to the front door to deliver to Karen the next time I went to her office.

Returning to the desk, I pulled open each of the drawers and withdrew their contents, giving them a cursory glance before placing them into a file box where they would be archived in case they were needed. There was little of interest: tidy collections of utility bills, statements for bank and credit card accounts, car service records, writing materials and stationery. The bottom right-hand drawer also contained a box the size of a large egg with a seam running around its middle. It was pretty, the shape pleasing, the finish a sparkly black lacquer. This I would keep, I thought. I shook it and something rattled within. The lid fit snugly, and I wriggled it off. A flat, two-inch-long key made of dull grey metal lay inside.

I studied the key for a moment. It was, if I wasn't mistaken, a safety deposit box key. No doubt, to a box in Leo's bank.

"It's not surprising," Karen said when I called to tell her about the key. "Most people have safety deposit boxes. I should have thought of it myself. Probably some savings bonds, that kind of thing. Or maybe some jewellery." She said she would arrange with the bank for us to access the box. Her secretary phoned within the hour with a proposed time to do so.

The last thing I went through was Leo's briefcase. Inside, I found documents related to his job, his laptop, and his cell phone. The laptop had been issued to him at work, and a quick perusal of the files on it confirmed that this was its main purpose. I set it and the papers aside to return to his former secretary. The cell phone was registered in Leo's name and, according to the contract I had found when cleaning his desk, had over a year of service left. I decided to keep it for my own use. The battery was dead, and after I recharged it and turned it on I found five messages waiting.

The first was from Leo's secretary advising him of a cancelled meeting. The second was from a colleague regarding a matter he wanted to discuss during the Christmas party at which we had never arrived. The third was from a bookstore to say that a book Leo had ordered had come in.

The fourth message did not make any sense. I played it again and listened carefully. The male caller spoke with a foreign accent.

"*Oui, allô*," he said. "It is Jean-Marie. I want to let you know that the trees, they are now down, and the men take them away. Please call me." Wrong number, I concluded, and deleted the message as I had done with the others.

The fifth message was from the same caller.

"*Allô?* It is Jean-Marie. I am sorry, but I do not hear from you so I am calling again. It is necessary to pay the men for cutting the trees, and for me and Dak also it would be nice to be paid. Thank you."

Poor guy, I thought as I deleted the message, *hope he eventually got paid.*

***

I dressed with more care for my meeting with Karen at Leo's bank. I had no alternative to the toque, so I pulled it on, vowing to go shopping for something more stylish after the meeting.

Karen was waiting for me in the bank's concourse, a glass cavern that stretched high overhead and sent the sharp crack of our heels on the marble floor ricocheting through the hard-edged space. At the reception to the safety deposit box department, Karen asked for the person with whom she had made the arrangements for us to access the box. A man with close-cropped silver hair wearing a paisley bow tie and navy sweater vest led us to the vault with the safety deposit boxes and found the one Leo had rented. He and I inserted our respective keys, and when the door opened he withdrew a long, narrow box, carried it to a small room to the side, and set it on a table.

"I'll leave you to it. Call me when you are done," he said, and departed.

"Well?" Karen said, motioning to the long grey metal box. "Go for it."

I lifted the lid of the box. All it contained was a plain white envelope.

"As I thought. Probably some bonds," Karen said. "Do you want to have a look at it here or back at my office? I will have to keep it until probate is completed."

"There's no point in my going to your office," I said. "I'll just open it here."

I drew the envelope out of the box and turned it over. Nothing was written on either side. The flap was sealed. I upended the envelope to shift the contents down, tore the top end off, and withdrew a folded sheet of paper.

"It's not a bond," I said, glancing at Karen.

I unfolded the paper. When I read what it contained, a chill spread like ice water under my skin. In Leo's slanting, spiky scrawl, a single sentence had been written: *In the event of my death, contact William Lord at Cawston, Lord, and Wortman in Surrey.*

***

By unspoken agreement, Karen and I entered the first café we encountered outside the bank. I don't know who was more shocked, she or I.

"I thought I handled all his legal affairs," Karen said, white-mouthed.

I was more bothered by the message's ominous tone. "Why would he do such a thing?" I said. "What could it mean?"

Karen couldn't seem to get past the question of violated loyalty. "Whatever it means, I don't know why he couldn't have trusted me with it."

I put down my cup of coffee. "I guess we should contact the fellow he mentions." I pulled the sheet of paper out of the pocket where I had stuffed it and glanced at it. "William Lord. Will you do it, or should I?"

Karen shook herself out of her funk and extended her hand. "That's my job. Let me find out what this is all about."

***

Karen called me the following day. William Lord had retired, she said, and Leo's affairs were now in the hands of another lawyer in the firm named Mohan Jasminder. She had set up a meeting with Mr. Jasminder two days hence. Did I want to attend as well? I said I would but declined her offer of a ride out to the suburb where the other firm's offices were located.

Karen was late for the meeting, and Mr. Jasminder, or Mohan, as he insisted I call him, and I filled the ten minutes we waited with small talk. Mohan informed me that he was the newest member of the firm, a fact attested to by the size and location (next to the noisy photocopy room) of his office and his smooth cheeks and eager manner. I learned that he had never met Leo, never even spoken to him. William Lord had distributed his clients among the other lawyers in the firm, and Leo was assigned to Mohan because his requirements were not complicated. This was reassuring but not informative. I asked whether Mr. Lord might be willing to talk to us, in the event that we needed some history of his dealings with Leo. Mohan thought that he probably would. but it would have to wait until he returned from his round-the-world sailing trip.

At that point Karen arrived, flustered. She had gotten lost in Surrey's unfamiliar streets. Refreshments were offered and accepted, and only after we were settled with our cups of tea and coffee did business begin.

The work the firm had done for Leo was mostly conveyancing until nine years previously when it had created a holding company to simplify the management of his investments and matters such as taxes. Karen and I glanced at each other: A company? His investments? Karen shot off a series of questions that Mohan, now very serious and slightly nervous, answered as best he could. He could provide few details beyond the fact that the holding company was managed by a financial services company. He wrote out the name, address, and contact person at this company.

"Did you know about any of this?" Karen said as we were leaving Mohan's office.

I shook my head.

"What the heck was Leo playing at?" she wondered.

We agreed that Karen would follow up with the financial services person to arrange a meeting before getting into our respective cars for the trip home. Karen drove off first, turning in the wrong direction at the intersection. She would, I suspected, be late for her next meeting.

***

As it was the end of the week, we were not able to meet with the person at the financial services firm until the following Tuesday. This gave me ample time to brood over Leo's newly disclosed affairs. I concluded that as the investments predated our involvement, there was really no reason why he needed to tell me about them. I certainly hadn't kept him up to date on the status of my meagre savings account. As for Karen, Leo had honoured his commitment to be her first client but apparently hadn't felt obliged to seek all the services he needed from her. There was, perhaps, some baggage there. In all, it was perfectly explainable. Except for the bleak note Leo had left with its troubling sense of foreboding.

***

The next day, I was wheeling a cart around the supermarket when Leo's cell phone rang. Only my family and Karen knew the number, and I answered expecting to hear one of them.

"*Ah, oui, allô?*" It was the voice that previously had left two messages on the cell phone's voice mail.

"You've called before, haven't you?" I said. "I think you have the wrong number."

"I am calling for Leo. This is not his number?"

I carefully put the cantaloupe I was holding down. "You were calling for Leo?"

"Yes … Is it possible to speak with him, please?"

I swallowed. "Leo is, ah … Leo passed away. Several weeks ago. In a car accident."

A long silence was broken by a sigh at the other end of the line. "I am very sorry. It is why he did not call, *n'est-ce pas?*"

"Who is this?"

"Ah, yes, my name is Jean-Marie Lebeau. You are Leo's wife?"

What had I been to Leo? "Sort of," I said. "You left messages before. I'm sorry, I thought that you had called the wrong number. What is it you wanted with Leo?"

"I work for him, you see, and there is some money to be paid."

"Where are you?"

"I am on South Salish."

"Ah, yes." The property Leo had bought and neglected to tell me about. "What have you been doing? You mentioned something about trees."

"Yes, it is for the vineyard."

"The *what?*"

"Well, maybe it is not a vineyard yet …"

I didn't speak for a moment. "I know nothing about this."

"I am sorry," Jean-Marie said, "but we are working since three months, and there is no pay for a long time."

26

"I—look, don't worry. I will make sure that any outstanding bills are covered."

Jean-Marie's sigh of relief was audible. "That is very good. For me it is not so bad, but Dak, he does not have very much. And the men who cut the trees and take them away, they are not very happy."

"I need more information," I said. "Can you send me the bills? I will give you my address."

"Yes, but maybe you can come here to South Salish? It would be more quick and, now, I do not know what to do."

***

Karen and I drove separately to the office of the financial services firm that managed Leo's holding company, also located in Surrey. She must have consulted a map, because I arrived to find her at the entrance speaking on her cell phone. She smiled a greeting, issued some final instructions to, it sounded like, her secretary, and slid the phone into her purse.

While we waited in the reception area, I brought Karen up to date on my conversation with Jean-Marie Lebeau. "I'll need some money to pay what's owing."

Karen was silent for a moment. "Well, Leo certainly had his secrets. But, yes, I will set up an account and release some funds."

Scott Mayo, the person we were to meet with, arrived and led us to a conference room. Scott was short and seal-like, slightly wider at the hip than the shoulder and dressed in a sleek grey suit. He said that Maria Sawatsky, from a sister company that managed properties, would also be joining us, and she arrived shortly after. Maria was a woman in her late forties whose playful pageboy hairstyle belied her perpetual scowl. We all sat down, and Scott and Maria slid two sets of buff folders full of documents across the table for Karen and me. They then each gave a summary of the assets held by Leo's company. Scott covered the financial investments, securities, bonds, and other instruments. Maria reviewed the real estate portfolio, a collection of diverse commercial and rental properties in the metropolitan area. Scott explained that the revenues from the real estate were used for expenses or invested. He handed Karen and me a single sheet. It was the valuation Karen had requested. Scott cautioned that with the limited time they had had to prepare the valuation, the figures were notional and a more thorough review would be needed to arrive at an accurate figure. Regardless, the total at the bottom of the page shocked Karen and me into silence. The value of the assets held by Leo's company was estimated at over eight million dollars.

We ended the meeting on the agreement that Scott and Maria would continue to oversee their respective parts of Leo's portfolio. Before going our separate ways, Karen suggested that she and I meet when we had both had a chance to absorb the information Scott and Maria had provided.

"That could take a very long time," I said, still shaken by what I had learned.

There was nothing in what Leo had ever said or how he had lived to suggest that he had this kind of wealth. The news had also rattled Karen.

"I had absolutely no idea," she said several times.

I wondered, again, whether it had been she or Leo who had decided they were better off being just friends.

***

On the morning I was to leave for South Salish, I packed for what I hoped would be a short visit. When I asked Jean-Marie Lebeau to recommend a place for me to stay on the island, he replied that there was a house on the property where Leo had stayed. The phone rang while I was rooting around in the kitchen for a plastic bag in which to wrap a pair of moccasins. I was running late and considered not answering it, but after four rings I snatched up the receiver and said hello.

"Who is this?" a man said. His voice had a slight accent and sounded like gravel shaken in a tin pan. I recognized the voice of a long-time smoker.

"It's Clare."

"You Leo's wife?" The words were threaded by a reedy wheeze.

I sighed. "Something like that. Who's calling, please?"

"Name is Nick Duvall. Did Leo ever mention me?"

"No. Should he have?"

"Well, maybe. He owes me a bunch of money."

Probably someone else owed money for some work, I thought. "Have you spoken to Scott Mayo or Maria Sawatsky?"

"Who the hell are Scott Mayo and this Sawatsky woman?"

"If it's payment for a job, they can take care of it."

"That's not what this is about."

"In that case, you may be better off talking to my lawyer." Had Karen become my lawyer?

"I don't think that would be a very good idea."

"Then I really can't help you."

"Now, listen here ..."

I glanced at my watch. "Look, I'm sorry, I've really got to go."

"Don't you hang up, bitch!"

I had had enough of Nick Duvall and clicked the handset into its slot. Apart from anything else, I didn't like being called names. I went to the bedroom, tucked the moccasins into a small suitcase, and zipped it closed. When the telephone rang again, I ignored it. The phone fell silent after the fourth ring. *Probably bumped to voice mail,* I thought. A minute later, it rang again. I gritted my teeth; there was no way I was going to answer it. Silence, again, after the fourth ring. Maybe he'd get the message.

I carried the suitcase to the entrance and opened the hall closet door. An Arctic front was threatening, and I looked for something suitably warm to wear. I spied David's anorak, which I had forgotten to return, and was pulling it off its hanger when the phone began to ring again.

"Enough!" I said. I walked over to the telephone and yanked the plug out of the wall. Standing in the blessed silence, I breathed deeply for a few seconds, then went back to the closet and shrugged on the anorak. I also put on Dave's duck boots and the toque, which I hadn't managed to replace. I slung my bag over my shoulder, picked up the suitcase, and walked out the door.

Chapter 4

The ferry was scheduled to leave at two o'clock. I had little experience using the ferry system, with its multitude of routes and vessels, and wanted to arrive at the terminal in enough time to find the right boat. When I cleared the edge of the city, a few fat, lazy raindrops hit the windshield. I accelerated to the speed limit, and the drops filmed the glass. I turned on the wipers, and as the blades swept across the window panic gripped my throat and my heart tripped around my chest. I swerved across a lane of traffic to the shoulder and braked hard. My car fishtailed and lurched to a stop. I shut my eyes and leaned my forehead against the steering wheel. Images flashed through my mind: driving rain, two hard, bright lights drilling through the rear window, the relentless swipes of windshield wipers, and fear. *What is this all about?* I thought, gasping. Was I beginning to remember the crash? I prayed not.

When my heart finally slowed, I took a deep breath and started the car up again. The windows were steamed over, and I rubbed the condensation off the windshield in front of me. A glance at the dashboard clock indicated that I was running seriously late.

My ferry had started to load when I arrived at the terminal. Fifty-fifty chance of getting on, the woman in the ticket booth said. My car and the car behind me were able to make it, but a glance in my rear-view mirror indicated that the last three did not. I followed the other passengers up the narrow metal stairs from the car deck to the lounge and settled in a seat by the window. The ferry shuddered out of its berth, laboriously turned around, and headed out to sea. It was raining in earnest now, and the drops streamed sideways across the glass. I watched them, mesmerized, until my eyelids drooped and I dozed.

What felt like a collision jolted me awake. We had docked at a small terminal. I craned my neck to see the signage; it wasn't the one I wanted. South Salish Island would be the last of the four at which the ferry would stop. A turbaned gentleman sat in the seat across and one over from me. He was in early middle age, with elegant features and large dark-lashed eyes. He wore a quilted jacket and jeans, but the feet he had propped up on the seat next to me were bare. They were very nice feet, clean, well-manicured and smooth. The man smiled at me, and I smiled back but, unsettled by the vague eroticism of his naked feet, I collected my bag, apologized for disturbing him, and left.

An hour and a half later, we reached South Salish Island. All the people remaining in the lounge got up to leave, and I followed them down the steps to the car deck. I had found a map of the island on the ferry and was able to trace the route to the property. The rain had turned to snow at some point, and when I drove off the ferry a white dusting covered the ground.

After one wrong turn, I found the correct address marked in faded letters on a worn board nailed to the gate post of an unprepossessing entrance. I turned in and drove towards a structure that loomed about three hundred feet up the driveway. I assumed it was the house Jean-Marie mentioned, the one Leo had stayed in, but when I drew up to it, I found an unfinished building, the walls raw plywood, the door and window openings nailed over with boards. Closer inspection confirmed that it was uninhabitable.

I had left the car door open when I got out and swore mildly at the snow that had quickly settled on the driver's seat. From what I could see, the driveway continued, and I drove along slowly, leaning forward over the steering wheel to see through the thickening snow. The road started to climb, and my tires skidded on the slippery surface.

The peril of my situation struck me. Here I was, in the middle of a snowstorm, spinning my tires on an unknown trail on my way to what I hoped would be shelter for the night. I stomped on the gas and my little Honda hatchback squirted forward, cresting the top of the hill and sliding to a skater-like stop beside what looked like a cabin. I turned off the ignition and got out. Jean-Marie had said that he thought Leo had kept a key hidden on a ledge under the eaves of the porch roof, and I hoped he was right, because I didn't fancy breaking a window to get in. Which I was going to do one way or another. In this weather, I wouldn't be going anywhere else this night.

The porch was a covered space about ten feet long and six feet deep recessed into the side of the cabin. It had a window with a closed blind on the facing wall and a door with a bronze knocker shaped like a dolphin to the right. The ledge where the key was supposed to be was a couple of inches beyond my extended hand. Leo would have just been able to reach it. I scouted around the cabin in the semi-dark for something to stand on, my eyes blinking against the driving snow, and found a ceramic pot lying on its side. It was too heavy to carry, so I rolled it to the porch, levered it up the steps, and flipped it upside down. It gave me the extra height needed to reach the ledge, and after groping along several feet of gritty wooden surface, I finally found a key.

The door stuck when I turned the doorknob but yielded to an urgent push, releasing a rush of dank, musty air. I found and flipped a light switch just inside. A rustic light fixture illuminated the small vestibule I had entered. Another switch farther inside lit up a large room with a vaulted ceiling. A kitchen with a full, if somewhat dated, complement of avocado-green appliances was tucked into one corner. A dining area, defined by a small wooden table and four spindle-legged chairs painted brown, filled another. Beyond the table was a set of French doors that opened to the outside. A sofa covered by a green and orange Indian print blanket centred in the room faced a black iron woodstove, next to which sat a few sticks of split wood on a jute sack. A messily folded newspaper lay on a wood laminate coffee table by the sofa. I checked the date: December third of the previous year. No doubt the date of Leo's last visit. I had been in Milwaukee then.

A short hall to the left led to two bedrooms and a bathroom. The back bedroom was empty. The one in the front contained a new king-size box spring and mattress set, bare except for a single pillow with no cover and a sleeping bag. An upturned wooden crate served as a night table and held a white gooseneck lamp, a small shortwave radio, and several suspense novels with loud, glossy covers, the kind Leo had called brain candy.

My breath streamed out in the damp chill. I dropped my suitcase and bag on the bed and went in search of a thermostat. There was none, but I discovered floor heaters under the windows in the dining room, bedrooms, and bathroom. I turned them all on, and they came to life with creaks and pops and the odour of burnt dust. There was no place to store the clothes I had brought, so I unpacked only my toiletries and deposited them on the bathroom sink counter. I was relieved to see a couple of towels on the rack, as it had not occurred to me to bring any. Nor had I thought to bring any food, I realized.

The kitchen cupboards held a few cans of hearty soup and baked beans, some soda crackers, a small bag partly filled with barista-quality ground coffee, now, no doubt, a bit stale, a French press coffee maker, and two each of cups, bowls, and plates. One drawer contained a similar complement of cutlery, a can opener, and a knife. A second had a box of matches, a flashlight, a set of keys, and a buff file folder. The file contained utility contracts. *No doubt some money owing there as well,* I thought, and closed the drawer.

I heated a can of chowder in a small saucepan that had been sitting on one of the stove's elements and sat down at the table to the modest meal. When I was through, I washed the bowl, pot, and spoon I had used. The rising wind fluted through hidden holes in the house, and branches scraped against the windows. I walked to the French doors, cupped my hands around my eyes, and peered outside. The air was now choked with snow, and it had drifted into crescents on the outside door and window sills. The windows rattled and the wooden beams creaked as the cabin shifted against the gale. The lights suddenly flickered, then went out. They came on again, but for only a second, like the flash of a camera. I breathed out slowly, willing the electricity to come back on. It didn't, but my eyes adjusted to the dark. The falling snow glowed in the rectangles of the French doors, and by this faint light I picked my way back to the kitchen and felt for the drawer that contained the flashlight.

In the short time they were on, the heaters had taken the edge off the cold, but the cabin was still far from being warm. I set the flashlight on the coffee table with the cone of light pointing at the iron stove and tried to start a fire. Dredging up memories from my Girl Guide days, I arranged wood and crumpled newspaper in the stove's sooty box. I struck a match and ignited the paper. The flame nibbled on the paper, reducing it to a crisp black cinder, then died. I added more paper and tried again with the same result. Two more unsuccessful attempts used up the remaining newspaper.

I shut the stove door with an exclamation of disgust, rose stiffly, and picked up the flashlight. *How long would the batteries last?* I wondered. I returned to the kitchen for a more thorough search of the drawers in the hope of finding some candles; there were none. There was really nothing to do but go to bed.

After performing my evening ablutions as best I could without any water, I crawled fully clothed into the sleeping bag and switched off the flashlight. I turned on my side, pressing my cheek against the pillow. It held a faint, familiar scent that I recognized, after a second, as Leo's. I sat up, my involuntary cry echoing in the cabin. I held myself, sobbing dryly. After a minute, I pressed the button on the flashlight and by its thin light groped in my shoulder bag for the bottle of painkillers the doctor had prescribed, for when it really hurt. I shook a tablet free and swallowed it. When I turned the flashlight off, the instant black dissolved into a dense grey with the pale squares of the bedroom window providing an eerie focal point. I lay down again, nestled my head in the pillow, and drew comfort from this residue of Leo's being.

***

When I woke the next morning, the snow still fell, but lightly, like sifted flour. The air was bone-chilling cold, and I stayed in bed, wrapped in the sleeping bag, trying to read one of Leo's thrillers. To ration the limited food supplies, I skipped breakfast, and my stomach twisted in anticipation of the can of baked beans I had promised myself for lunch. When I finally rose to dish out this feast, I noticed that it had stopped snowing. I was on my last mouthful of cold beans when the sound of the refrigerator motor lifted me out of my chair and sent the spoon I was using clattering to the floor.

A hot coffee warmed me enough to venture outside. My car was an anonymous white lump, and the snow lay a foot deep on the ground, all tracks on the driveway obliterated. I wouldn't be going anywhere soon. The cabin was marginally more comfortable, with running water and the growing warmth, and the radio's chatter took the edge off the isolation, but I studied the three remaining tins of food with dismay. Tomorrow I would have to walk down to the road and try to get into the town for provisions.

Late in the evening, I heard what sounded like a handful of rice being tossed on the metal roof. It took me a moment to recognize the sound for what it was: rain. In a few minutes, the scattering of rice had turned into a cascade of gravel. Throughout the night, the hammering of the rain on the metal roof broke into my sleep.

By morning, the rain had reduced the snow to a sea of slush and the sun shone blearily. I was jumpy with pent-up energy and decided to explore. The cabin sat in a small clearing ringed by a stand of cedar, fir, and arbutus trees. The driveway that my little car had struggled to climb disappeared through an opening at the left. On the right, the land dipped into a gully then rose into dense forest. The trees in the front were tall, their lowest branches high. Beneath them was a tangle of vegetation above which patches of bright blue sky shone through. The sky drew me, and I picked my way through the undergrowth.

I cleared the trees and gasped. It had been too dark when I had arrived to see the features of the property that now lay before me. I was standing on the edge of a shelf formed by a massive granite outcropping that projected out like the bow of a ship. About seventy feet below lay a talus of fallen rock, beyond which stretched a slope scarred by recently upended stumps and woody debris, no doubt the remains of the cut trees that Jean-Marie Lebeau had mentioned. It looked like a war zone.

Farther out, I could see meadow, and in the distance a valley rising to a line of hills with the highway I had driven in on threading through it. I stood for several minutes surveying the scene, then retraced my steps and followed the driveway down towards the unfinished building, which was about halfway to the highway. It was built into the slope falling away from the driveway, with the result that the basement was a full storey high on the lower side. The wood siding was weather-beaten, and the yard around was overgrown with bramble and weeds. Continuing on towards the highway, I found, at what would be the lowest spot in the field, a small pond.

I backtracked to the base of the granite outcropping. Some primordial upheaval had caused a rift in the ground, thrusting up the cliff. The different geological strata on its face showed clearly, the lines angling down to the right until the rock was swallowed by the ground. Over time, soil had accumulated on the shelf that was formed and a forest was born.

I continued past the base of the cliff and came upon a few rough-hewn posts connected by strands of rusted barbed wire that staggered over a rise and out of sight. I tracked the fence for a few feet, but a loose wire caught my ankle and brought me down on my hands and knees.

Pushing myself off the ground, I disentangled my foot and surveyed my muddied knees and hands with dismay. I rubbed my palms against my jacket and continued along the barbwire fence for several hundred feet until it joined the one establishing the boundary with the downhill neighbour's place at right angles. The neighbour's fence was almost my height and sturdy, made of wire knotted into six-inch squares. On the other side I could see animals grazing, several sheep and a llama. The llama sauntered up to the fence, meditatively chewing its cud.

I had once heard that llamas were inclined to spit when annoyed, so I kept a close eye on the one next door as I walked on. So intent was I on the animal that I didn't notice the little stone hut until I was almost upon it. The hut was about fifteen by twenty feet, the walls constructed of rocks of various sizes cemented together with a grainy grout. It sat in a small hollow surrounded by creeping vines. A man stood outside it, bent over a plastic basin set on a plank supported by two sawhorses. His dark shaggy hair grazed his shoulders, and all he wore was a pair of grey long johns, the elastic waistband torn from the fabric at the spot one would grasp to pull them up. His splashing in the water must have covered the sound of my approach because when I called out a greeting, he whipped around and yelped.

"Sorry," I said, "I didn't mean to surprise you."

The man was flagrantly hairy, his face obscured by a bush of a beard and his chest practically clothed in shaggy black fleece. He tucked his hands in the thicket of his armpits in an attempt to cover his nakedness and stared at me with comically round eyes.

"Are you Jean-Marie?" I said.

The man shook his head, grabbed a green and grey striped towel, and backed into the doorway of the hut until all that was visible was the gleam of his eyes. I hesitated a moment, then continued on, discomfited by the odd encounter.

The sheep had come up to the fence and now followed me, bumping along on the other side in a mass of dirty wool. After a couple of hundred feet, a cross fence stopped their progress and they bleated in protest when I left them behind.

The neighbour's buildings, a newer, ranch-style house, small barn, and two outbuildings, were towards the front of their property. One of the smaller buildings had a mesh enclosure at its front where a number of grey, white, and rust-red chickens scratched and pecked. Two border collies rushed up barking and tracked my movements on their own side of the fence. I left the dogs at the corner where the properties met the highway. On my side, the fence reverted to rough posts and strands of barbed wire. I followed it to the driveway at the far end of the property.

Having completed the circuit of the place, I returned to the cabin and collected my car for an expedition into the town. When I returned a couple of hours later, there was a blue pickup, not new but clean and undented, parked near the unfinished building. As I pulled alongside, a man leaning against it straightened up and walked towards me. I rolled down the window but kept the car running.

The man was in his late thirties and of medium height with large brown eyes and wavy chestnut hair that curled around his ears. He wore jeans, a brown aviator-style jacket, the leather showing the fine craquelure of long wear, and a navy fisherman's cap.

"Hello, I'm Clare," I said. "You must be Jean-Marie."

"Yes. Dak said you were here."

"Ah, that must be the fellow with the beard. I didn't know he lived on the property."

Jean-Marie folded his arms. "He lived in a tent in the park, and when the winter came it was wet and cold. Leo said it was okay."

I nodded.

"You did not say when you were coming," Jean-Marie said.

"No." I left it at that. "Why don't you come up to the cabin, and we can talk."

I had a head start on Jean-Marie and had put away the deli lasagna and pre-made salad I had bought for my dinner and had set a pot of water on the stove to heat by the time he knocked on the door. When I opened it, he stepped back in surprise; my height often has that effect on people.

"Come on in," I said, and turned back to the kitchen, leaving Jean-Marie to follow.

He hesitated in the living room, turning the fisherman's cap in his hands.

I motioned to the table. "Have a seat. I'm about to make some coffee. Would you like some?

"Yes, thank you." Jean-Marie pulled one of the chairs away from the table and sat down.

The water had started to simmer, and I busied myself with the French press. "Oh," I said turning to Jean-Marie, "I haven't any milk or cream."

"That is okay."

When the coffee was ready, I poured it into the two cups, set them on the table, and sat down. "I don't have any sugar either. Sorry."

Jean-Marie hesitated briefly but picked up a cup. "It does not matter," he said.

We studied each other briefly, warily. "I brought some cheques to pay you and Dak, and for the tree-cutting."

Jean-Marie's brow lifted, and he sat back in his chair. "Ah, that is good. That is very good. Thank you."

"Was it necessary to cut down those trees? The place looks pretty awful right now with the stumps and everything."

Jean-Marie sat forward again. "We decided, Leo and me. It is the best place for *les vignes*."

"Well, clearing it up is a priority."

"Now that there is money, yes, we can get the trucks to take it away," Jean-Marie said. "Also, there are other things to do."

I sighed. "I know nothing about any of this, about how it happened or what the plans were. How, for example, did you get involved? Did you know Leo before?"

Jean-Marie took a sip of coffee and grimaced. He set the cup down and shook his head. "No. Only when he buy this place. When I first see this hill, it is five years now, I say to Jasmine, she is my wife, I say it is perfect for *les vignes*. Then when it is put for sale, I come to visit and walk around. Many times. But I do not have the money to buy it. So I say to Richard, he is the agent, when someone buys this land, tell them that they can make a vineyard and I will help them. It was many years, but then Leo came, and he bought it just for that, to make a vineyard. And he hired me to do it."

"It all sounds so implausible," I said.

"*Peu plausible? Pourquoi?*"

"I mean, is it warm enough?" I recalled reports on grape-growing in the interior of the province, but the climate there was desert hot. "It's pretty cool out here on the coast."

Jean-Marie shook an admonitory finger at me. "No, no, not too cold, I think." He gestured towards the windows. "That is south, it catches the sun. And here, it is on a hill." He bent his arm to indicate the angle. "It makes the heat stronger."

I sat without speaking for a long moment. "I'm not sure where we go from here. Yes, we need to clean up those stumps but, then, I don't know ..."

Jean-Marie pushed his coffee aside and leaned forward. "But it is all planned, it is what Leo wanted."

This man bothered me, his presumptive familiarity with Leo, their understanding, the plans they shared, all unknown to me. "Well, I'm not Leo."

"No, *bien sûr* ..." Jean-Marie's shoulders sagged.

"And I need to think about whether I want to commit to a vineyard. To begin with, I don't know the first thing about growing grapes."

"No," Jean-Marie said, "but I do."

***

Before he left, Jean-Marie casually mentioned that the blaster who had blown up the large tree stumps had initially used too much explosive and debris had landed in the neighbour's yard.

"What? Was anyone hurt? And the animals, are they okay?" I envisioned tree stumps raining down on the sheep and the llama.

"No, no, it was the other neighbour, and just on the grass. They did not mind too much."

"I think that I had better talk to them," I said. All I needed was a lawsuit. The day's unaccustomed activity had tired me, so I left the task to the following morning when, shortly after nine o'clock, I knocked on the door of the green house on the uphill side of my property. A woman answered the door. She had an elfin look that made it hard to pin down her age, but the silver threads in her dark cap of hair and laugh lines on her heart-shaped face suggested that she was in her forties.

"Hello, I'm from next door ..." I jerked my thumb in the direction of my property. "I want to apologize for the business of the stumps' being blasted into your yard. I just found out about it yesterday."

The woman's face lit up in a smile. "You must be Clare," she said. American, I thought. From somewhere south.

"Yes. I guess Jean-Marie mentioned me."

"Actually, we knew about you from Leo." Her smile faded. "I was very sorry to hear about him."

"You knew Leo?"

"Yes, he stayed with us a few times while he was buying the property, then he visited whenever he came out after."

"I see. Had you known him before?"

"No. He needed a place to stay, and our house was convenient." The woman gestured at a small wooden sign attached to a post at the front gate that I had passed by but not noticed. It said "Southern Comfort B&B." "We became friends. Hugh, in particular, enjoyed Leo's visits. We were thrilled to hear what he was doing." The woman glanced over her shoulder than back at me. "I'd ask you in for a coffee, but I've got some guests to see off and Hugh's not quite up yet."

"That's okay," I said, backing out the door. "Sorry, it *is* a bit early."

The woman followed my retreat out to the front step. "No, no, we'd love to have a chance to visit. How about later this morning, say, eleven?"

I agreed and headed back down the walk.

"Oh, by the way, my name is Kate," the woman called after me.

I acknowledged the introduction with a wave.

Jean-Marie had arrived while I was talking to Kate. He and Dak were standing by the unfinished building, and I walked over to greet them. Dak melted away when he saw me approach, but I figured he was just embarrassed about being caught in his underwear. Jean-Marie said he would be meeting with a heavy equipment operator shortly to arrange to remove the stumps and clean up the logged land.

"Good," I said.

"Also, Jasmine and I, we thought maybe you could come and have dinner with us tonight. Before you go away."

My goodness, I thought, *here only a few days and already a social butterfly.* I wasn't sure I wanted to become friends with Jean-Marie in the circumstances, but it would have been churlish to refuse. Jean-Marie wrote out directions from a page torn from a small coil notebook he had in his pocket, and I continued on my way.

***

At eleven o'clock I returned to the green house. Kate let me in and led me through the entrance hall, which had a set of stairs leading to the second floor and French doors opening to rooms on both sides, to a large room that ran across the back with a long pinewood table on the left and to a showcase kitchen on the right.

Kate pulled out a chair at the table, next to a tall man seated at the end. "This is my husband, Hugh," she said. "Darling, this is Clare from next door."

Hugh's handshake was not limp, but neither was it strong. I understood why immediately. The chair he sat in was a wheelchair, and his navy turtleneck sweater hung loosely on his frame. His sandy hair was white at the temples, and deep lines of illness etched his face. His eyes were the colour of cornflowers and burned as though the power that his body had relinquished had pooled there. I was caught in their intense scrutiny for a long moment.

"I was very sorry to hear about Leo," he said. "I enjoyed our talks very much."

I nodded my thanks and sat down. Kate set a cup of coffee in front of me, and I selected a banana muffin, moist and fragrant, from a basket she offered.

"I'm so glad you're here," Kate said. "We had planned to have Christmas dinner with you and Leo, and when you didn't come out we wondered if … well, if something had happened between the two of you. Leo had mentioned that you were away for much of the time."

I swallowed the mouthful of muffin I had been chewing. So this is where Leo had planned to bring me for Christmas. The destination was a secret, he had said, and when I had protested that I had to know what to pack, he told me I wouldn't need much.

"I didn't know we were supposed to come here for Christmas. In fact, I didn't know about this place at all."

Kate smiled. "Well, it was supposed to be a surprise. Leo told us that this was your Christmas present."

I slowly set the half-eaten muffin down on my plate, my appetite gone. I thought of the preparations Leo had made at the cabin for our Christmas visit—the brand-new bed, the two plates and two cups, the two forks and knives and spoons—and my heart twisted. Tears threatened, and I swallowed hard.

"I had no idea," I said, my voice shaky. "It's beyond anything I could have imagined. I don't know why Leo would have wanted to give me a vineyard."

"He said it was something you had wanted to do," Kate said.

I fiddled with my muffin. Where had Leo ever gotten the idea that I wanted a vineyard? Kate and Hugh exchanged glances, then Kate smiled and remarked on how different the slope looked now with the trees gone.

"Yes," I said, relieved at the change of topic. "It's a bit of a mess now, but Jean-Marie has arranged for someone to clean it up." The rest of the visit passed in general chatter. I asked polite questions about how the southern belle that Kate's accent suggested she once had been had ended up here on South Salish, and heard the story of how she and Hugh had met in Houston where he worked for an oil company. They returned to Hugh's home in Canada when he was diagnosed with multiple sclerosis and settled on South Salish, where they had spent their honeymoon. The bed and breakfast business gave them something to do and a chance to meet people.

"My mother can't believe that I take in complete strangers," Kate laughed, "and she's appalled that I feed and clean up after them."

After a suitable time, I made my excuses and got up to leave. Kate saw me to the door. "I'm sorry if we've upset you," she said. "And if we were too personal. It's just that Leo spoke of you so much we feel we know you."

"It's okay," I said. I thanked her for the coffee and left. I puffed back up my driveway, remarking to myself that the sojourn in the country was helping me recover my strength. When I paused at the end of the steepest section to catch my breath, something jiggled in the depths of my memories then burst into my mind.

When Leo and I had gone to San Francisco last year, we spent a day touring wineries in Sonoma and were at our fifth stop, sitting on the patio outside the tasting room, enjoying the spring sun. On Leo's advice, I had tried to spit out the samples of wine we had been offered, but as many went down my throat as into the spit bucket and I was feeling decidedly mellow. In the expansive way one speaks in that condition, I had rhapsodized about the beauty of the rows of vines, bushy and bright with early growth, converging towards the horizon, and the appeal of the lifestyle they implied, proclaiming that growing grapes would be a much more authentic existence than churning out abstract analyses of dysfunctional organizations. Leo hadn't promptly said, *Great, why don't we do it?* He hadn't said much at all, only, I recalled now, that the vineyards near his village were one of the few things he remembered from his time as a child in Italy.

"Oh, Leo," I whispered.

45

***

My stay on South Salish was turning out to be longer than I'd expected, so that afternoon I headed into the small village on the island to stock up on provisions and household items. By the time I had returned, unloaded, and set up some of the new items, it was time to get ready for dinner at Jean-Marie's. I hadn't packed for going out, and the best I could do was a pair of clean jeans, a black turtleneck sweater, and the moccasins I had brought to wear in the cabin. I tucked the moccasins in the pocket of Dave's anorak and looked at myself in the mirror. My hair, now a half inch long, was singularly unflattering. I sighed and pulled on the brake and muffler toque.

"No, that's okay, I'll keep it on," I said to Jasmine when I arrived at her and Jean-Marie's house and she offered to take the toque.

"Whatever you like," Jasmine said, and turned to hang Dave's anorak on a peg that sat just inside their front door.

Jean-Marie and Jasmine's house was an older two-storey building painted daffodil yellow with white trim on an acreage cut out of heavy forest. An old barn sided with vertical planks of silvery cedar and a small outbuilding painted a cerulean blue with white trim sat a distance from the house. The whole place had a ruthlessly cheery aspect.

When Jasmine had answered the door, a little boy, four years old or so, peered curiously at me from behind her long, loose black skirt. "This is Michel, but we call him Mischa," she said, after introducing herself. "Jean-Marie is finishing dinner. Come on in."

I followed Jasmine to a large country kitchen fitted with what looked like the original cabinetry refreshed with ivory paint. Jean-Marie was at the stove stirring something in a cast iron Dutch oven. He looked up and smiled a greeting. Gorgeous spicy smells wafted up from the pot, and my mouth watered.

"Have a seat," Jasmine said, motioning me to a wooden pedestal table covered with a dark blue and green batik cloth that stood in the centre of the room. I pulled out one of the chairs at the table and sat down.

"Wine?" Jasmine said. I accepted, and she filled two glasses with red wine. "Jean-Marie?" she said, waving the bottle.

"No, *merci*," he said. "Later."

Jasmine brought the glasses of wine over, handed me one, and sat down on a chair across the table. She raised her glass. "*Santé.*" I nodded and took a sip from my own, conscious of Jasmine's scrutiny.

I was quite accustomed to not being the prettiest woman in the room but had rarely felt as outclassed as I did in Jasmine's presence. The word that popped into my head as I looked at her was "luscious." Her skin was deep caramel, her hazel eyes were slightly slanted and fringed with long dark lashes, and her hair spilled down her back in a cascade of ebony curls. She wore a fitted scarlet blouse against which her breasts strained for release. I tugged self-consciously at my toque.

No one spoke. I took another sip of wine for courage and said, "So where are you from?"

Jasmine raised her eyebrows. "Right here." She lifted her chin. "Why do you ask?"

Off to a great start, I thought. "With Jean-Marie's accent, I just assumed ..."

Jasmine glanced at Jean-Marie, who was setting thick white plates and cutlery at each of our places. "Yes, he's as French as they come, but my great-grandparents settled this land. Refugees from the Civil War. They came up from the States via the Underground Railroad. My family may not have been in the country as long as yours, but we're bona fide Canadians now."

"Actually, my parents came in the 1960s," I said mildly. "So where did you and Jean-Marie meet?"

"In Senegal. I was there searching out my roots and studying the kora," Jasmine said. "You know the kora?"

"Yes," I said. My father once had invited an impecunious visiting musician who played the multi-stringed instrument indigenous to West Africa to stay with us. Seydou had appropriated our living room as his personal space for three weeks, hanging washing on the lamps to dry and strewing his belongings—sandals, clothes, books—around the room. He had eaten raw peanuts constantly and absentmindedly dropped the shells on the shag carpet. Remember how hard it was to clean those rugs? After he had left, my mother spent hours crawling around the living room, picking bits of shell from the carpet, and swearing under her breath.

Jasmine's eyes widened when I mentioned Seydou's name. "He's considered one of the grand masters now." She paused for a moment, then continued, "Jean-Marie said that you may not go ahead with the vineyard."

So that's what this dinner was about. "That's right. I still haven't decided what I'm going to do."

Jasmine toyed with her glass. A man might have found something of interest in the way she slid her fingers up and down the stem, but it was lost on me. "Well, then, when do you plan to make up your mind?"

She had moved her fingers to the rim of her glass and was raising a thin line of sound from it. I recalled running out of the room whenever my father put his album of glass harmonica music on the record player, and I didn't like the sound any better now. I gritted my teeth.

"I'm not sure," I said.

Happily, Jasmine abandoned the glass and leaned back in her chair, hooking an arm over the back. By some miracle, the buttons on her blouse did not pop. She gave me a direct look and said, "Jean-Marie left a good job to take this on for Leo. It's not that easy to find steady employment on this island. Maybe landscaping is not as exciting as a vineyard, but he's guaranteed work for most of the year and the pay is decent."

Jean-Marie set plates of grated carrot salad on the table and said quietly, "*Ça suffit*, Jasmine." Jasmine pouted but didn't say anything more.

We got through the three courses of the meal—after the carrot salad, a lamb curry, and to finish, a pudding that tasted like next-day cream of wheat porridge with a strawberry compote on top—making polite conversation. When the dishes had been removed to the sink and coffee poured, Jasmine took Mischa, protesting, off to bed.

Jean-Marie and I sat in an awkward silence for several moments until finally I spoke. "Jean-Marie, this business of planting a vineyard, it's a hard decision. If Leo were still here ... but on my own, I don't know."

"It would be the same like if Leo was here," Jean-Marie said.

"Tell me, why does planting this vineyard matter so much to you?"

"Ah." Jean-Marie pushed his coffee cup to the side. "The vines, they are in my blood." His fingers touched his chest lightly. "I grew up with them, in France, *la Côte Chalonnaise*."

"What happened? Why are you not still there?"

Jean-Marie turned his hand out in a helpless gesture. "Many things change. I could not stay. I went to the south. There was a man from Algeria with a vineyard, and I went to work there."

"They grow grapes in Algeria?"

"Yes, of course." Jean-Marie went on to explain that he spent five years bringing a neglected vineyard back to life and productivity. "But, you know, not very good wine. I was *découragé,* and I left."

After leaving Algeria, Jean-Marie spent a year wandering through North Africa and West Africa. When he reached Senegal, his savings were almost depleted and he knew that soon he would have to return to France.

"But to go where, and do what, I did not know," he said.

One evening, he went to an open-air music festival in Dakar.

"There was a lady playing the kora. The lady was Jasmine." Jean-Marie shrugged as though no further explanation was needed. And, indeed, it wasn't.

After they married, Jean-Marie followed his wife back to Canada, initially to Montreal, then to South Salish, when Jasmine and her sister inherited their grandmother's property.

"It is like that." Jean-Marie said in conclusion.

It had been a difficult disclosure from someone I sensed was a very private man.

"I understand now," I said.

Jean-Marie nodded, his face inscrutable.

I rose from the table. "Still, I must think about this. Let me have the weekend, and we can talk on Monday."

***

I spent Saturday morning trying to figure out what to do about the vineyard. Before I had left his house, Jean-Marie had given me a sheaf of papers that, he explained, contained the plan and budget he had prepared for Leo. The information was well organized, divided into several sections containing numbered points. It was, however, written in the loopy and, to me, almost indecipherable handwriting common to Europeans, and I had to transcribe the numbers into a set of tables to understand them better. Even so, without some kind of framework to evaluate them, I had no basis on which to make a decision.

I need to talk to someone, I thought, and dialed my parents' telephone number. They knew about my inheritance, but not the full extent of it nor many details. It would, I knew, shock them more than anything, and I still wasn't sure how I felt about it myself. I brought my father up to date on the South Salish property.

"And there's a fellow all ready to go ahead and plant a vineyard. What do you think I should do?"

My father didn't speak for a moment. "That sounds very complicated and ambitious, Clare," he said. "You suffered a very serious injury, and not that long ago, and I think the most important thing right now is for you to rest and fully recover."

He's probably right, I thought, hanging up the phone. I shrugged on Dave's anorak and set off for a walk around the property. Maybe it would have some answers for me. I was almost at the highway when I heard my name called.

"Hello again!" Kate waved at me from her side of the fence, a cigarette glowing between her fingers. I walked over to where she was standing.

Kate crushed the stub in a metal jar lid sitting on the fence rail. "Hugh doesn't like me smoking. I've given up trying to stop, but I'm down to four cigarettes a day. This is the one I have with my mid-afternoon coffee." She held up a ceramic mug with a sea green glaze in her other hand. "I just made a fresh pot; do you have time for a cup?"

"Why not?" I said, and smiled.

Despite the awkwardness of my last visit, I liked Kate and Hugh. And it might be a chance to bounce around the idea of the vineyard. Hadn't they said that Leo had discussed his plans with them? I contemplated vaulting over the fence, something I had often done in my teens, to get to Kate's but settled on the longer and more decorous route out the front gate and via the highway.

Hugh opened the door to me, and I followed his wheelchair to the wooden table. I accepted a cup of coffee and a cookie lumpy with nuts and raisins and chunks of chocolate. I took a bite. It was still warm from the oven and a treat after the canned lentil soup I had eaten for lunch.

"Delicious," I breathed.

Kate put a cookie on a plate and passed it to Hugh. We chatted about this and that, and at one point Kate mentioned how exciting it would be to have a vineyard next door and how much their guests would enjoy it.

"The thing is, I'm not sure whether to go ahead now that Leo's gone," I said. "For one thing, I know absolutely nothing about growing grapes. About growing anything, for that matter."

"But you have Jean-Marie. And think of how much fun it will be to learn," Kate said. "I couldn't even boil water before we moved out here, right, darling?" Hugh shrugged and smiled.

"I barely know Jean-Marie. There are lots of unknowns, in fact."

"But wouldn't it be boring if you knew everything about it?" Kate said.

It was clear what she thought. I wondered at her insistence. She was about to speak again when Hugh, who had me fixed in his tractor-beam gaze, said, "I think Clare needs time to decide what to do."

The doorbell rang while Hugh was speaking, and Kate rose to admit a middle-aged couple whom she introduced to us as the Croydons, guests at the B&B for the next couple of days. When she left to show them to their room, Hugh leaned forward.

"There's no rush to make this decision, Clare."

"I can't leave Jean-Marie hanging. He left his other job to do this. Leo made all kinds of commitments to him and to Dak."

Hugh cleared his throat. "If it's a question of money, Kate and I may be able to help."

I shook my head. Money was the least of the problems. "Thanks, but that's not an issue. I'm a city girl and this ..." I gestured vaguely in the direction of my property. "It's all so foreign."

"Well, I can't say that we won't be disappointed if you don't proceed, Clare, especially now that the trees are cut down, but you should do what makes you most comfortable. But if we can help in any way, just let us know."

The Croydons had come back downstairs, and Kate was taking them through some materials about local attractions on South Salish. It was a good time to leave, and I did.

I was no further ahead the next day, feeling, if anything, more confused with Kate and Hugh now added to the list of people who would be disappointed if I cancelled the vineyard plans. Cranky weather that alternated window-rattling winds with lashing rain kept me indoors brooding. I thought of the Croydons and their plans to tour the island's artisan studios.

Late in the afternoon, Melanie telephoned to scold me for leaving for South Salish without telling her. "I've been calling your place all week, but all I got was the message that your mailbox was full," she said. "I even dropped by on Friday to make sure you were okay. It wasn't until I talked to Mom this morning that I found out where you were. What are you doing out there, anyway?"

I told her about Leo's intention to plant a vineyard and the difficulty I was having deciding whether to go ahead or not.

"Don't be silly," Melanie said. "Whatever would you do with a vineyard?"

That was, I think, the point when I decided to proceed.

***

The next morning I called Karen, and when we eventually spoke I explained what I was going to do and asked how soon money could be made available. She said she would make arrangements for a line a credit for me to draw on, explaining that the probate of Leo's will would take a while to complete because of tax complications related to his properties and securities.

"Sorry to keep bothering you with all this stuff," I said, by way of thanks.

"It's no problem, Clare. It's my job. And you pay me well for it."

Of course I do, I thought as I hung up the phone.

I gave Jean-Marie the news later that morning, observing that planting the vineyard would be an act of faith, not logic. Trying not to smile too broadly, he nodded and shook my hand, and we were in business. We discussed some practical details, then he walked me around the property, pointing out the attributes of the site as they related to the planned vineyard.

One of the things he liked best was that the property was in the middle of a hill. In France, he said, the middle of a hill was considered a better location for a vineyard than the top or bottom. He also liked the cliff, which he called *la falaise,* explaining that the rock would absorb and retain the sun's heat and then slowly release it, warming up the environs. When we reached the pond, our arrival produced a series of discrete plops as the frogs we disturbed jumped into the water.

"So that's the source of the noise I hear at night," I said.

When the sun went down the frogs started singing, and I could hear their croaks all the way up to the cabin at the top of the hill. The banks of the pond were thickly overgrown, and it seemed to be swallowing itself. Weeds growing from the bottom floated leaves up to the surface.

Jean-Marie walked to the edge and looked around. "It will need to be made bigger," he said.

We turned and looked back up the slope we had descended. The goal, Jean-Marie said, was to get some vines into the ground in the fall. These vines would have the benefit of the winter rains to get well established. We would plant the remaining vines next spring. By the third year, we should get half a crop; by the fifth year, a full crop. I had seen the numbers indicating that there would not be much income for several years and shrugged. It was not, at the end of the day, why we were doing this.

In the meantime, other tasks needed to be done. Jean-Marie kicked at a pile of bean-sized pellets on the ground. "The first thing is to put up a wire fence for the deer," he said, describing the perimeter of the farm with a broad sweep of his arm. "They will eat everything."

"Are there any plans for this building?" I said, as we passed by the unfinished structure. "It's quite an eyesore."

"*Ah, oui,* Leo said it is for the winery."

"The *what?*" I said. "There was no mention of one in the plans."

"Not now, but later," Jean-Marie said airily, and moved on. I hurried after him, wondering just what it was that I had signed up for.

Chapter 5

When I returned to Vancouver a few days later, Leo's condo greeted me with what felt like a studied neutrality. *Oh, it's you,* it seemed to say. I kicked off Dave's duck boots and hung up his anorak. I picked up the handset of the telephone on the hall table to call Melanie and tell her I was back, as she had insisted I do. There was no dial tone, and after a moment's puzzlement, I recalled yanking the cord out of the wall before I left. When I plugged it in again, the message light lit up and flickered. As Melanie had said, the mailbox was full, but all that had been recorded was a series of clicks. I voiced a rude word and cleared the mailbox.

After unpacking, I made a cup of coffee and took it to the living room. The light switch controlled a series of table lamps, and when I flicked it on the room filled with a subdued glow. I stepped into the room and stopped short. Something was wrong. It took a few seconds to identify the anomaly as an empty space in the wall unit where the stereo components had been. Someone had broken in while I was away.

I set my cup of coffee down on a side table and examined the spot where the components had sat. All that remained were a jumble of wires and neat rectangles of dust. I wasn't familiar with the technology but understood from Leo that the components were ultra-high-end units. I turned slowly around. Nothing else seemed to be missing. A survey of the remainder of the condo indicated that none of the art, by far the most valuable of the household items, or my few bits of jewellery had been taken. The only other place that appeared to have been touched was the desk in the den. I recalled leaving the files that Mohan Jasminder, Scott Mayo, and Maria Sawatsky had given me neatly stacked on the right-hand corner. They were now scattered across the surface. But nothing from the desk had been taken.

It took several hours for the police to respond to my call, and the young constable who eventually did made a note of what had been taken in a perfunctory manner. When I remarked on this, he flipped his notebook closed and said, "You're lucky they took only the stereo stuff. Usually they rip off anything—computers, jewellery, even clothing—they think they can sell quickly." He shook his head. "Often, they make a mess of the place was well. Probably just one guy, and it was all he could carry."

"But why here?"

"You were gone, right? Maybe someone knew. Maybe someone just checked doors to see which locks were the easiest to pick." The policeman waved at the door. "The kind of doorknob lock you have isn't that complicated."

"But the main door to the building is locked. You wouldn't think we'd have to barricade ourselves in here."

The constable raised his eyebrows and said, "Listen, if a person really wants to get in, all he has to do is wait for any of the residents with a key and sneak in behind them, or follow them into the garage."

"So, basically, the building isn't secure at all."

"Yup," the constable said. He cautioned that it was unlikely the stolen items would be recovered and strongly advised that I install a new lock. I said I would, and when the door closed behind him, I slid the small hall table across it.

Rather than being reassured by the fact that only the stereo components had been taken, I wondered about the select nature of the theft. It did not seem to be random, a desperate junkie looking for easy pickings. Had some acquaintance known about and envied Leo's system and taken the opportunity of my absence to lift it? And why the interest in the files on the desk?

***

The next morning, I found a store selling all manner of security devices and selected a state-of-the-art electronic lock controlled by a number pad instead of a key. One of the store technicians came by the following afternoon to install it. The telephone rang while he was giving me the final instructions on the lock's use. I ignored it, and it stopped as it usually did after four rings. When the phone started to ring again, the technician said that he thought I had gotten the hang of the lock, twisted his ball cap around from back to front, and headed down the hallway to the elevator whistling. I set the printed material he had left on the side table and hurried to the phone, catching it on its last ring.

"It's about time," a man said in response to my greeting. "Where've you been?"

"Who is this?"

"It's Nick Duvall."

Nick Duvall. Where had I heard that name before? "Yes?" I said.

"This is Clare, right?"

"Yes?"

"We talked a couple of weeks ago. You hung up on me."

I recognized the gravelly voice as that of the smoker who had called just before I went to South Salish. The one who had probably left all the clicks on my voice mail. "I didn't hang up; I just wasn't able to help you."

"Yeah, right. By the way, nice place you have."

"Wha…?" I swallowed. "You're the one who broke in here."

Nick Duvall snorted. "With that chickenshit lock you had, it was hardly breaking in."

"What were you looking for?" I struggled to keep my voice steady. "What do you want?"

Duvall's voice hardened. "Leo owed me. He had my money, and I want it back. In fact, I figure there should be some interest owing. That stereo stuff was a start."

"It's not that simple," I said. "First of all, what proof can you offer of this debt? Second, I don't have access to Leo's money yet. If he did, in fact, owe you something—"

Nick let loose a salvo of obscenities, and I jerked the phone away from my ear.

I swallowed and continued, "The thing is, it's not mine yet. If Leo owed you something, it could take me a while to pay it back."

"I don't got *a while*. I need it now."

"And what if I can't get it to you now?"

"That, sweetheart, is a possibility you don't really want to consider."

"I really think you need to speak to my lawyer."

"Oh, no, no, no." I could hear the finger shaking at me. "No lawyers. Lawyers are bad news. Just you and me."

"But ..."

"Look, sweetheart, I don't like telephones too much. We need to have a nice tête-à-tête about this."

"I don't think—"

"Maybe I should drop by your place again."

I pulled the telephone away from my ear and stared at it in horror. Duvall's voice continued to issue from the earpiece in a tinny string of sound. I put the handset back against my ear. "Wait," I said. "Wait. We can meet somewhere." The need to keep Duvall away from the condo overrode concerns over the validity of his claim. I cast around for a spot that had lots of people around. "How about the Starbucks in the Waterfront Centre mall?" It was the place where I used to get my morning coffee on the way to work, and it was always busy.

"Where the hell is that?"

"Oh, you're not from here?"

"Never mind that. Pick somewhere easy to find."

"You know Robson Street?" When Duvall grunted that he did, I said, "There's a Starbucks on the corner where it crosses Thurlow." This would be even better: It was one of the busiest intersections in the city.

Duvall snorted. "You guys and your fucking coffee. Whatever. When?"

I exhaled slowly. Might as well get it over with. "How about tomorrow morning, say, ten?"

"Yeah, sure."

"Wait, there are actually two Starbucks there, cater-corner to each other," I said. "But there's a building on one of the other corners with a clock tower. It's easy to see. It would probably be better if we met under the clock tower so you don't get confused."

"Takes a lot to confuse me," Duvall said.

"How will I know you?"

Nick rasped out a laugh. "I've got a red jacket. Got tired of wearing clothes with no colour."

"Okay."

"And, sweetheart, no funny business." The phone clicked, and the call was over.

***

What the ...? I breathed, as I hung up the phone. I sat down hard on the kitchen chair. Who the heck was Nick Duvall, and whatever could Leo have had to do with him? Duvall's manner was too rough for him to have been one of Leo's colleagues, and it was unlikely that someone like him would have been a friend. What could Leo have possibly owed him money for? Was he someone else, like Jean-Marie, who had done work for Leo somewhere? Would I find yet another surprise like South Salish and Leo's holding company with all its investments?

And there was the matter of the break-in. I rose and went to the bowl on the table at the entrance, into which I had dropped the card of the policeman to whom I had spoken about the theft. I flicked it with my thumb for a few seconds and then put it back. No funny business, Duvall had said. I'd hear him out, and if whatever debt Leo owed him was reasonable, I'd pay him off either from the vineyard line of credit or, if necessary, my own money. I did not want this man anywhere near my home again.

***

The next morning, I arrived at the clock tower a few minutes early. I figured that I might be able to gain some advantage by catching sight of Nick Duvall before we met. People flowed around me, and I looked left and right, scanning the crowd. I felt surprisingly relaxed; we would meet, we would talk. The calm dissolved when, despite my surveillance, I felt a tap on the shoulder and the gravelly voice said, "You must be Clare."

I turned, shaken. "How did you know me?"

"You're the only one standing around. Everybody else is moving."

Nick Duvall was a couple of inches shorter than I. His coal black hair was threaded with grey and needed a cut, and his cheeks showed the vestiges of an adolescent case of acne, but neither detracted from his striking good looks. He wore a red wind jacket over a black T-shirt and jeans that hadn't yet lost their dye. He raked me with a raw, frankly sexual look, a little smile playing with his mouth. My face reddened under his scrutiny.

"That from the accident?" Duvall said, gesturing to the surgery scar that still was visible under my cropped hair—I had had to abandon the toque when a stitch had caught and it had unravelled.

"Yes," I said.

Duvall pointed to a ragged white line about two inches long that clipped his left eyebrow. "That's what I got."

It took me a moment to understand the implications of what he had said. "It was *you* who was in the car behind us? *You* hit us?"

Duvall scowled. "I was just trying to make a point. Can't help it that stupid asshole couldn't drive. Didn't do me much good, did it?"

I gaped at Nick Duvall, my mind buzzing in disbelief. "But, why?"

Duvall jerked his head in the direction of the Starbucks. "Let's go get that coffee." He took a step toward the crosswalk. "Let's go," Duvall repeated, his voice hard. He tried to take my arm. I made an inarticulate noise and shrugged him off but followed when he moved to the edge of the sidewalk.

The crowd waiting to cross the street bumped and jostled around us. When the light turned green, Nick Duvall and I surged onto the crosswalk in the midst of the mass of people, neither of us speaking. We had just passed the centre line when Nick stumbled against me and clamped on to my shoulder. I tried to jerk free, but he caught my arm with his other hand. He stopped walking and turned, eyes wide with surprise, to me.

"What are you doing?" I said. "Let me go!"

We were now stationary in the crosswalk, the tail end of the pedestrians scurrying around us.

"We have to go!" I said, trying to free myself from Nick's grip.

His hand slipped from my shoulder as his body sagged. The traffic lights changed, and the cars at the front of the lanes we were blocking honked their horns. Nick had sunk down and fallen backwards, dragging me down with him, his grip on my arm still tight.

He's having a heart attack! I thought, as I crouched over Nick. He lay on his back, one leg bent under him. His eyes searched mine and he tried to speak, but his words were lost in a gurgle of blood. The horns continued, sharp and intolerant.

I motioned to the people waiting at the corner with my free arm. "Help me! Something's happened!"

A couple of people whipped out cell phones and started punching in numbers. A young woman stepped onto the crosswalk and waved her arms at the cars in the lanes behind us. "It's an emergency!" She ran to us and knelt down. "I'm a nurse," she said. A young man, apparently her companion, had tentatively followed her and hovered nearby.

Nick's grip on my arm slackened and his hand slid to the ground, but his eyes still held mine as though he was willing me to answer some unknown question.

"They're calling for help," I said. I slipped my hand under his head to cushion it.

"That's a really awkward position. He must be uncomfortable," the nurse said. "Let's try to turn him on his side."

I wondered about the wisdom of moving someone in Nick's condition but deferred to her medical authority. She slid her hand under one of Nick's shoulders and raised it. "Aaargh ...," she said. I noticed for the first time that she had curly carrot-coloured hair pulled back in a ponytail and the flushed red complexion that often accompanies it. Her pale green eyes were wide with surprise.

"What is it?" I said.

The nurse didn't speak but shifted position, her free hand busy at Nick's back. When she pulled it back, Nick drew in a fractured breath, then his eyes lost focus and he exhaled in a puff and a trickle of blood. His head was suddenly heavy in my hand. I stared down at his inert face. *So that's how it is,* I thought.

The nurse was jabbering something, the sound bouncing off the roaring in my ears. I looked up; the front of her purple sweater was covered in blood, and she held up a knife with a short black handle and slender blade. There was a lot of noise after that—sirens, and horns, and people calling out, and, in what could have been minutes or hours, a couple of policemen arrived, followed shortly by an ambulance crew. They pulled me away, and I sat on the curb, my arms folded on my knees, my head down, my eyes closed.

Sometime later, I was bundled into a police car, driven to their headquarters, and taken to a room. A policewoman asked me some questions—the who, what, where kind—to which I mumbled some replies. The nurse who had helped also had been brought to the station and was sitting at another desk, this one in an open area visible through the glass walls that enclosed the room I was in. She still wore the purple sweater, the blood stains now an ugly brick colour, and her pale green eyes bulged with shock. Her male companion, who had hovered but not helped, was arguing with two officers nearby.

After some time, a hand appeared at my left side and set a bottle of water down in front of me. "We meet again," a soft, seductive voice said.

Chapter 6

"Okay, so run me through it one more time," said Inspector Yuen.

And I did. How Nick Duvall, one of Leo's friends whom I had never met before, had called and we had agreed to meet for a cup of coffee. How we had been crossing the street in the middle of a throng of people when Duvall suddenly collapsed. How I had no knowledge of how he came to be stabbed; I hadn't even known that it was what had brought him down until the nurse had withdrawn the knife.

It quickly became apparent that my presence during Nick Duvall's murder made me the prime suspect, so I did not tell Inspector Yuen about Duvall's role in the car accident, his breaking into the condo, his claim that Leo owed him money, or anything else that would suggest I had a motive for his death. Whatever Duvall had done, he was now beyond justice. I, on the other hand, was in a very tricky position.

Inspector Yuen finally released me in the afternoon with warnings that I would be required for further questioning and shouldn't leave town. I stumbled down the front steps of the police station and looked around, dazed. A passing cab responded to my feeble wave, and I had almost reached the condo when I remembered my car parked at a meter three blocks away from the corner where Duvall and I had met. I redirected the cab and, after it had delivered me to my car, plucked some parking tickets out from under my windshield wiper and then wove an unsteady course home.

Inspector Yuen called the next morning to invite me back for another chat. I had sunk a good portion of a bottle of Leo's Laphroaig scotch the previous evening, cutting it with only a chunk of cheese and a few crackers, so I put off Yuen until later in the day when, I hoped, my wits would be sharper. When I sat down at his desk, his questions came from an unexpected direction.

Why had I not mentioned when we had previously spoken that Nick Duvall had been released recently from the Prince Albert penitentiary?

If my stammering protestations that I didn't mention it because I had absolutely no knowledge of Duvall's history didn't convince him, I hoped that my dropped-jaw surprise at the news did.

"Why, again, did he want to see you?" Inspector Yuen said.

"I really don't know," I lied, trying to corral my scattered thoughts.

"So how did Leo know this Nick Duvall?"

"I have no idea. Leo never spoke of Nick Duvall." I was grateful, on this matter at least, to be able to speak the truth.

"Then why would you meet with him, a total stranger?"

I sighed. "Look, why not? He asked, and I agreed. It was just for a cup of coffee."

"Don't you think it's curious that this guy pops up out of the blue, and wants to meet with you?"

I didn't reply for a moment. Finally, I said, "What's curious is that one moment you can be driving to a party and the next you're fighting for your life. Compared to that, Nick Duvall's wanting to talk to me wasn't particularly odd."

Yuen's eyes flickered, but he pressed on. "Okay, well, let's say, 'Isn't it curious that when you meet this guy who calls you out of the blue, who you don't apparently know, someone sticks a knife into his back?'"

"That's what happened, yes, but I don't think it had anything to do with my meeting with him." I was suddenly struck by the thought: *Did it?*

Yuen was speaking again. I swung my attention back to him. "Sorry, I missed what you said."

"I was wondering if you can think of any reason why someone would want to kill Nick Duvall."

I spread my hands in exasperation. "As I said, I didn't know him at all, so I can't even begin to speculate who might want to kill him or why."

"And you had no reason to?"

I opened my mouth to speak, then shut it. Inspector Yuen and I locked gazes for a long moment. It helped that I was starting to get very annoyed at his persistent and circular interrogation and that my head was still throbbing dully; otherwise, I would surely have succumbed to the panic that was nibbling at the edges of my mind.

"I have told you all I know about Nick Duvall, and there is really absolutely nothing more I can add," I said, in a voice so steady I almost convinced myself.

"And you're sure you don't know Phyllis Lesik?"

I had started to rise, and stopped halfway up. "Who on earth is Phyllis Lesik?"

"The supposed nurse who was holding the knife."

"I didn't know her name, and I took her word for it that she was a nurse. It was hardly the time to start demanding credentials. And as far as I can tell, she was holding the knife because she had pulled it out of Nick's back."

"Which brings us back to how it got there in the first place."

I finished standing up. "Look, there were people all around us. Someone in the crowd did it without anyone else noticing and just continued on. I wish I could help you, I really do, but there is nothing more I can say. And right now, there is somewhere else I need to be."

***

It took two weeks for the bruises left on my arm by Nick Duvall's dying grip to fade. During this time, I endured three more sessions in Inspector Yuen's office and one in the condo, which included a court-warranted search of the premises to look for links to Duvall. After my second conversation with the Inspector, I called Karen to see if she had any advice on how to deal with him. She suggested that I engage a criminal lawyer because the types of legal issues I was potentially facing were beyond her purview and said she could recommend a couple in her firm. When I protested that I didn't need a criminal lawyer because I hadn't done anything wrong, she told me not to be naive.

I survived Inspector Yuen's serpentine interrogations by sticking to the script I had created. Fortunately, the forensic analysis found no evidence that I had handled the knife used to kill Duvall, nor had the police search of my pockets and person turned up gloves or tissues that I could have used to protect my hands, had I done so. After grudgingly accepting this, Inspector Yuen tried to develop the notion that I was part of a joint action, that I had lured Nick Duvall out and set him up, and someone else had done the dirty deed then departed amidst all the confusion. He even tried to fit Phyllis Lesik, the ministering angel, into the scheme—we were, after all, each other's alibis—but this scenario collapsed under its own improbability. When Yuen finally stopped calling me, I breathed an enormous sigh of relief and hoped, fervently, that I would never have to speak to him again.

Chapter 7

I had first noticed the guy at my new favourite coffee bar, a place one
block from the condo that favoured Nordic jazz as its wallpaper music.
During the time when I was explaining myself to the police, I had
taken to having my mid-morning coffee and reading the newspaper
there. What had caught my attention was his tic: Every few minutes,
he would roll his shoulders as though working out a kink in his neck. I
had noted it over the course of one morning for its oddity and then
promptly forgot about it.

Later that week, I had stopped at the local grocery and was
selecting apples from an outside bin when I caught the shoulder
roll out of the corner of my eye. Turning, I saw that it was the
same bulky man with close-cropped blond hair from the coffee
shop. He even wore the same charcoal leather jacket that he had
had on before. This time, he was standing, hands in pockets, in
front of the window of the butcher shop two stores down,
studying the fine cuts of meat on display. Even then, I assumed
that he lived in the neighbourhood and wasn't surprised to see
him again.

The third time I saw him, late in the afternoon the next day, he was bent over a newspaper box just outside my condo building, ostensibly reading the headlines visible through the window. He still wore the grey leather jacket. As I passed him just before turning into the forecourt of my building, I remarked to myself that the guy really needed to expand his wardrobe. It wasn't until the entrance door clicked shut behind me that I wondered about seeing him yet again. I glanced back through the large foyer windows at the spot where he had been. He was still there, and he was staring at me.

The hair rose on the back of my neck. I dashed to the elevator, punched in my floor, and hammered the Close Doors button. Inside the condo, I leaned against the front door and hyperventilated. When my breathing had slowed to normal, I felt ridiculous. *So you see this fellow around, so what? It's just a coincidence,* I scoffed. *Maybe he was just looking at you.* Melanie had strong-armed me to Philip's salon again to figure out what to do with my scrubby mop of hair, and his solution was to load it with gel and comb it back into a slick pompadour. It made me look like one of those androgynous characters that populate German cinema and attracted a certain amount of attention, although, I had to say, mostly from other women. I walked jauntily to the closet to hang up my jacket. The doorbell rang.

I returned to the door and peered through the peephole. The man in the grey leather jacket stood outside, his high cheekbones broadened even further by the fisheye lens. I staggered back, my thoughts skittering around like mice. How did he get in? How did he know which condo was mine? The address board still showed Leo's name. That meant he either knew a lot about me or had made the connection between me and Leo. Was this another mysterious person from Leo's past? Was he in some way associated with Nick Duvall? The doorbell rang again. My hand drifted to my mouth. What do I do now? He saw me come in, he knew I was here, but there was no way I was going to open the door.

I heard women's voices in the hall, then a *tick,* like a small object brushing against the door. The voices grew louder; there was a burst of laughter. I put my eye to the peephole. Two women passed through the field of vision; the man was gone. I opened my door and peered out. One of the women was unlocking the unit two down from mine. The door to the stairway at the end of the hallway was slowly closing.

I ducked back into my hallway, grabbed my jacket and shoulder bag, and exited, quickly tapping in the code for my lock. I ran to the elevator and hit the Down button, glancing over my shoulder to the stairway door at the end of the hall. The elevator hadn't left the floor after the women had got off, so it opened immediately. I jumped in and jabbed the button for the parking garage. Through the gap between the closing elevator doors, I saw the stairwell door open and the man in the leather jacket emerge. Our eyes met for a second before the doors closed.

"Come on, come on," I said, beating my fist against the wall of the elevator as it descended. It stopped once on the way down, and again at the ground floor where the person who had entered got off. After what felt like an eternity, I reached the parking garage and raced to my car. I left streaks of rubber on the concrete floor backing out and turning, and when the metal barricade that secured the condo parking entrance finally rose, I pressed the gas pedal to the floor and bolted.

***

I drove without thinking to the ferry terminal and, finding myself there, took the next crossing to South Salish Island. It was already dark when I turned into the driveway of my property, and I had to brake abruptly to avoid ramming the gate. The gate? I got out to open it. It was two sections of heavy wire mesh connected by a latch in the middle. I pushed them apart, drove through, and closed them behind me.

The next morning, I woke with more than the usual sense of disorientation one experiences when sleeping in a strange place. Not that the cabin was unknown, but coming back to it was like entering another reality. Reflecting on my headlong flight from Vancouver in the clear light of morning, and at a safe distance from the condo, I wondered whether I had overreacted. There could be a perfectly simple explanation for the guy's being at my door. Maybe he was selling something, or was one of the religious door knockers. But if his presence was innocent, why did he leave when the women arrived? I remembered the brief moment when our eyes met before the elevator door closed, and I shivered. There was intention in his look, but of what?

After a meager breakfast, I decided to let Jean-Marie know I was there before heading to town for provisions. Outside, I noticed a new tall wire-link fence running along the driveway and behind the cabin, descending to the left along the edge of the gully that separated the cabin from the forest in the back. It hadn't been visible when I had arrived in the dark. Although no doubt necessary to keep out deer, the fence seriously detracted from the woodsy ambiance of the cabin's setting.

Jean-Marie and Dak were using a heavy chain attached to a bright red tractor (a purchase financed by the line of credit Karen had set up) to uproot some broom bushes. I said a quick hello and then left them to their work. I stopped next at the Southern Comfort B&B. The front door opened just as I was about to knock.

"… an absolutely wonderful time. We will certainly return and tell all our friends." The speaker was a woman with white hair swept up into a luxurious knot and wearing a crisply cut camel coat. She stepped through the door followed by a bald man in a khaki Barbour jacket. whose salt and pepper mustache was the size of a nailbrush, and by Kate, who carried matching Gucci bags.

I stepped away from the door to let the people pass.

"Clare!" Kate said, catching sight of me.

"Sorry, I should have called."

"No, no, what a nice surprise. Go on in. I'll be there in a minute." Kate hurried after the couple, who had descended to their car, a pearly blue Lexus sedan straddling the line of coloured pebbles that demarcated two parking spaces.

I entered the house. Hugh was at his desk in the office, and he glanced up when he heard me come in.

"Clare," he said, his face brightening. "I thought it was those awful people back again. Come in, come in!"

As Hugh and I were exchanging greetings, the front door opened and closed, letting in a sound fragment of car tires crunching on the gravel drive.

Kate came in and said, "Put them on the 'Sorry, we're all booked up' list."

"Yes, definitely." Hugh had turned to his computer and was bringing up a file.

"What's that?" I said.

"It's a record of the guests we never want to see again," Kate said. She motioned at the computer. "And anyone who says they were referred by them."

"But what was wrong with them?" I said. "I thought the woman said they had a wonderful time."

"Then it must have been from the pleasure of complaining." Kate threw up her hands in disgust. "Our place was too hard to find, the road was too rough, there were no restaurants nearby, the room was too cold, the frogs too loud, the bed too soft, the pillows too hard, the sticky buns too sweet, the eggs too runny. But, never mind. It's great to see you. Let's have a coffee."

Hugh and I followed Kate to the kitchen, where she poured mugs of coffee and set out plates and a basket of the sticky buns. I dug in without prompting.

"So when did you get back?" Kate said.

I sucked the tips of my fingers clean. "Last night."

"Lots happening at your place," Hugh said.

I shrugged. "I guess so."

We chatted about this and that, and after half an hour I rose, collected our dishes, and carried them to the sink. "Do you need anything in town? I have to go in to buy some clothes. All I have is what I'm wearing."

"Thanks, but I'm going in later for a major shopping," Kate said. "Did you forget your suitcase?"

"No, I ..." I stopped, conscious of where my explanation would take me. To that point, I had not discussed Nick Duvall's murder with anyone but the police, not wanting to worry my family with the strange business. I stood awkwardly, not knowing how to continue.

Kate had been pulling Hugh's chair away from the table. When I fell silent, she stopped. "What's up, hon? Everything okay?"

I cleared my throat. "The oddest thing happened when I returned to Vancouver. A man I was with was killed, stabbed, as we were crossing the street, and the police think I did it."

Kate and Hugh stared at me for a moment.

"Who was the man?" Hugh said.

I put my hand to my forehead. "It's all so weird."

Kate slowly pushed Hugh back to the table. "Why don't you tell us what's going on," she said.

I returned to the table, sat down, and told them about meeting Duvall and how he died.

"And you have no idea who Duvall was?" Hugh said.

"He apparently knew Leo, said he had some unfinished business with him." I told them about Nick Duvall's calls, his break-in, his claim that Leo owed him some money. "But I don't know how much or what for.

"And just before Duvall was killed, he told me he was the one driving the car behind us, the one that kept bumping ours. He said he was trying to make a point and didn't mean for the crash to happen."

"Oh, Clare!" Kate said.

"What did the police say about that?" Hugh said.

"I didn't tell them."

"You didn't? Why not?"

"Look, Hugh, I don't need you to scold me. This inspector was doing his best to arrest me for Duvall's murder, and I didn't want to give him any reason to do it."

We fell silent. Kate's and Hugh's expressions were hard to read: a mix of shock, curiosity—skepticism? Was I wrong to have confided in them?

I started to rise. "I should leave."

Kate reached across the table and caught my hand. "Clare, hon, are you running from the police?"

"No." I eased back into the chair. "I came here because I think someone is now after *me*." I described my encounters with the blond man in the leather jacket, his suspicious behaviour when he came to my door.

When I had finished, Hugh shook his head. "This is scary stuff. I really think you need to talk to this Inspector Yuen, put the police in the picture."

"But what can they do? And how do I know they'll believe me? Especially since I've held out on them to this point."

"The police may already know things about Nick Duvall that might shed some light on what's going on. And if someone else is after you, it's best they know. But, yeah, I expect you'll have some explaining to do."

***

Hugh's observation turned out to be an understatement.

"I should charge you with obstructing justice!" Inspector Yuen said when I went back to Vancouver to talk to him the next day.

I shrank back into my chair as he rose from his desk, but it was only to pace, three steps to the door to his office, three back to his desk. After a few turns, he sat down, picked up his telephone, and drummed a pattern on the number pad.

"Get in here," he said, and hung up. Even angry, his voice had a dreamy quality.

I was deeply regretting having taken Hugh's advice. Yuen had been livid when I filled him in on the details I had neglected to mention during his previous interrogations.

"Why didn't you tell me before?" he said, as we waited for whomever he had called.

"I was afraid you'd think I had a motive to kill Duvall and arrest me."

"And you're sure you didn't, in fact, do it?"

I laughed shakily. "What a funny way to put it. Yes, of course, I'm sure."

"And now you say someone is following you."

"Yes, well, I think so, anyway. I saw the same guy several times in my neighbourhood, and on the last occasion he came to my condo but then took off down the hallway when some other people came into view. As I was leaving, which was right away, because he scared the heck out of me, I saw him returning to my door. And he saw me."

Yuen tapped his lips with his steepled fingers and studied me without speaking. The door opened, and a younger officer who had been present when Yuen had previously questioned me entered.

"Get yourself a chair," Yuen said when the officer looked around for somewhere to sit.

The officer left the room briefly and returned with a molded plastic chair on skinny metal legs and then set it and himself down just inside the door. Yuen quickly summarized the new information I had provided. As he listened, the young officer glanced back and forth between Yuen and me.

"And now she says someone's after her." Yuen turned to me. "You know what I think? I think your boyfriend may have been involved in some tricky business."

I had been gripping the arms of the chair I was in and slowly opened my cramped fingers. So maybe Yuen wasn't about to lock me up. "What do you mean, 'tricky business'?"

Yuen gave me a look as if to say, *Are you putting me on, or just dumb?* "Something criminal."

My mouth popped open. "No! Leo wasn't like that."

"I think we need to find out more about Leo, what he'd been doing, have a look at his finances."

I thought of Leo's secret hoard of properties and money and felt a sudden chill. Could he have been involved in something illegal? "I don't understand why, with Leo dead," I said. "Especially now that you know Nick Duvall was responsible for the car crash."

Yuen rested an arm on his desk and leaned forward, his eyes hard. "Look, Duvall was killed, and we still need to find out who did it. With the connections you've just described between him and Leo, and now with the guy you say is following you in the picture, we've got to check out Leo's affairs. It sounds like they were all part of something bigger that's still being played out, and we may find some links, some leads, there."

This wasn't an outcome I had anticipated. Had I just opened up a can of worms?

Yuen noted my apprehension. "You got a problem with that?"

"No, no, I guess not. You'll have to talk to Leo's lawyer, though."

I accepted a pen and paper from Yuen and scribbled down Karen's contact information. When I pushed it across the desk, Yuen glanced at it briefly before passing it to the young officer.

"So what are you going to do about the guy who was following me?" I said.

"I can't do much without more specific information. If you see him again, let us know right away."

I started to object, but Yuen and the officer had risen from their chairs, so I had no choice but to follow. "Thanks, I'll do that," I said tartly, and left Yuen's office, nodding at the young officer who held the door open for me.

***

Outside the police station, I looked around with the sense that the world around me had shifted somehow. Was it possible that Leo had been involved with some criminals? Had there been a dark side to him, a covert life to which I hadn't been privileged? I thought of the gentle, generous man I had known for four years and shook my head to dislodge these disloyal thoughts.

I decided to head straight back to South Salish, where I figured I would be safe until whatever was going on blew over. On the way, I stopped at the condo to pick up some clothes. I parked two blocks away from the building and entered through the back door. There were a number of people coming and going through the lobby, and under the cover of their movements I emptied my mailbox and slipped into an elevator. At my door I stopped, momentarily stymied by the new lock. The entry code popped out of the pocket of my memory to which it had been consigned, and I tapped it in.

After packing a suitcase, I retraced my route out the back door and hurried down the street to where my car was parked. I kept my head down and my eyes on the sidewalk on the premise that if I couldn't see someone they wouldn't be able to see me. I eased my car into the street, and with a sigh of relief, headed for the ferry terminal.

Chapter 8

Two days later, I was up late reading when all of a sudden the frogs stopped singing. Now that spring had arrived, the occasional ribbit I had heard on my first visit had swollen to a full chorus. From time to time, they would fall silent when some nocturnal wanderer, a cat or a raccoon, strayed too close to the pond. I went back to my book, caught in the grip of the last pages. When I finished a few minutes later, I threw the book into a corner of the sofa, disgusted with the facile ending, and got up. Funny, I thought as I brushed my teeth, the frogs are still quiet. It didn't usually take this long for them to start singing again.

I was undressing when I heard a *crunch* on the driveway gravel outside the cabin. I stopped, my T-shirt halfway over my head, to listen. There was a second *crunch,* then a third and a fourth. I slowly lowered my T-shirt and stood, frozen to the spot, highly conscious of the fact that I hadn't locked the doors.

You know how your body is sometimes way ahead of your mind in responding to a situation? Well, mine decided it needed to get the hell out of the cabin, so I grabbed a sweater and my shoulder bag and bolted out through the French doors. In the house my movements and agitated breathing had covered any further sounds from the driveway, and I didn't hang around to listen for them once I was outside. I slipped around the side of the house, then took several unseeing steps in the dark toward the gully where I knew the new fence to be. The sky was heavily overcast, so there was neither moon nor stars to provide any illumination, and I held one hand out blindly in front of me as I shuffled forward until my fingers touched metal mesh. I felt my way along the fence, down the gully, and away from the cabin, curling my toes through my thin moccasins around the loose rocks and broken twigs to keep from slipping. There was an indistinct noise and what sounded like a bird calling somewhere behind me, and I picked up the pace, slipping and sliding on the dark and uneven terrain. The ground finally leveled out, and, without warning, I walked into the neighbors' cross fence where it joined the one I had been following.

I listened for a moment, but all was still. *Where to go?* I wondered. Not to Kate and Hugh's, because I would have to cross the property to get there and I didn't want to risk running into whoever had been crunching up the driveway. That left the other neighbours. I barely knew them, and it was well after midnight, but I had no choice; there was no way I would be able to spend the night outside. I started walking along the fence in the direction of the road. My eyes had adjusted to the dark, and I was able to move more quickly, but I trailed my fingers along the wire, for comfort more than for guidance. I recalled that the fence further along was lower than the six feet of wire that enclosed the sheep and llama, and it would be easier to climb over there.

I was approaching that juncture when I came across Dak's little stone house. I had completely forgotten about him. After a few moments' consideration, I stepped up to his door and knocked. There was no response, so I knocked again, hoping that the sound would not travel. A voice on the other side of the door demanded roughly to know who it was.

"Dak? Dak, it's me, Clare," I said in a loud whisper. After a short wait, the door groaned open. Dak was buttoning up a plaid shirt, and I realized that he had taken a moment to get dressed.

"Dak ..." I suddenly felt weak-kneed. "Can I come in?"

"Yeah, sure." Dak stepped back, and I took a few steps into his house. A flame flickering in a lantern that sat on a small table drew me forward. As the door closed, the flame flared up then collected itself into a small square of fire. I turned away from its mesmerizing light to face Dak, who was staring at me without speaking.

"I'm very sorry to bother you at this hour, but someone was about to break into my cabin, and I left." Dak made a move towards the door. I put my hand on his arm. "No, no, not a good idea to go there now. Really, all I need is somewhere to stay tonight. Could I maybe, uh, stay here?"

After a moment, Dak nodded, secured the door with a wooden latch, and came into the room. I looked around for the first time. A small wood stove anchored the space, its black pipe angling up through the ceiling. It emitted warmth and the pleasantly acrid smell of hot resin and wood smoke—the smell I had come to associate with Dak but never previously identified. I went to the stove and held out my hands.

Apart from the table and a small stool tucked underneath, an orange and gold flowered armchair, the rocking kind that bobbles on a base like a Christmas tree stand, and a wide wooden bench along the opposite wall, most of the other furniture consisted of wooden fruit crates arranged in various ways to store clothes, dishes, pots, and provisions. A piece of plywood balanced on two crates held a two-burner Coleman stove. Hats and outerwear hung on a series of pegs over the bench.

Dak was at a narrow bunk pushed against the far wall, shaking out the pillow and smoothing the coverlet. "Here," he said, motioning to the bed.

I raised my hands in protest. "Ah, no. Please. I'll be fine in the chair. Just a cover, if you have an extra one."

"No, you take it. I can sleep on the bench." Dak went to the stove, opened the door of the firebox, threw in a hefty log from a box full of them, and stirred up a shower of sparks with a metal poker.

"You take it," he insisted when I protested again.

I nodded agreement and gingerly stepped across the room, shrugged off my shoulder bag, slipped off my moccasins, and crawled under the coverlet on the narrow bed. Dak rummaged in a crate tucked under the bench and drew out a patterned sofa pillow and a coarse grey woolen blanket with a thick black strip along the border. He wrapped the blanket around himself like a cloak, cupped his hand over the lantern to blow out the light, and shuffled over to the bench. He shifted around for a few moments, getting settled, then fell silent and, after a few minutes, judging by his light snores, asleep.

I lay in Dak's bed, the bedclothes still warm from his body, enveloped in the smell of resin and wood smoke. *I'll never fall asleep,* I thought, and promptly did.

***

The smell of brewing coffee, and an urgent need to relieve myself, woke me. I swung my legs out of the bed and tugged on my moccasins. After wishing Dak a good morning, I asked him where to find the bathroom. He nodded in the direction of the door, not meeting my eyes.

Whatever, I thought, and went outside. The heavy dew seeped through the thin leather of my shoes as I hurried along looking for a private spot. I found one behind a muscular broom plant, pulled down my jeans, and crouched, moaning with relief. My presence had brought the sheep to the fence, and they huddled there, watching me.

"Oh, for Pete's sake," I said, zipping up.

I returned to Dak's hut to find a basin of warm water, a sliver of soap, and a towel resting on a sawhorse trestle that sat outside. I splashed my face and soaped and rinsed my hands.

Dak came out and set a mug of coffee next to the basin. "Got sugar, but no cream."

"Black's fine," I said, folding up the towel. I curled my fingers around the cup. The coffee was piping hot, and I inhaled the steam. I followed Dak back into the hut, where he was setting out unmatched plates with thick slices of charred toast, knives, a tub of margarine, and an economy-size jar of supermarket raspberry jam on the table. Dak glanced up from the slice of toast he was smearing with jam. He drew the stool out from under the table and motioned me to the spot. "You sit here." He carried his own plate of toast and cup of coffee to the orange and gold armchair and lowered himself into it carefully, his arms held out for balance.

I sat down and dressed my own piece of toast. When I bit into it, it had the familiar yet exotic character that an everyday food eaten in a foreign locale acquires. Four more bites, and it was gone. I licked the lingering sweetness from my lips and wiped my hands on my thighs. Dak had found the point of balance in the armchair and was calmly munching on his toast, for all the world like he regularly treated women to breakfast. Maybe he did; what did I know?

As I drank my coffee, cooler now and with a metallic edge from having been boiled, it struck me that Dak had offered his hospitality without question, had asked for no explanation beyond the brief one I had given him when I arrived.

"Dak, I can't thank you enough," I said.

Dak swallowed the last of his toast, brushed the crumbs from the pelt on his face, and said, "It's okay."

"And I was wondering, if it's not too much trouble, do you think you could come back with me?"

"Sure." Dak set his empty cup down on the bench, bent over the side of the chair, and tugged a heavy fisherman's sweater out from one of the crates under the bench. He rose and pulled the sweater over his head. "If you're finished, we can go now."

We set off across the property to connect with the driveway. In the light of day, I had the horrible sense of having overreacted again, that what I had heard was simply some animal on its nocturnal wandering. To prevent my looking foolish when we found the cabin undisturbed, I said, "It may have been nothing, but, you see, I think someone was following me in Vancouver, and I thought maybe it was them, you know, creeping up in the middle of the night."

Dak stopped abruptly and looked at me. "Someone's following you?"

"I think so. In the city. I thought I'd be safe out here on the island, but maybe they've found me."

Dak looked at me for a moment longer, then glanced around, walked over to some debris, and pulled out the broken limb of a tree. It was almost three feet long and as thick as my wrist with a jagged end. Dak hefted it and nodded. "Let's go," he said, and strode on, his shoulders raised, his arms bowled out, the improvised club gripped in his hand. Not knowing whether to laugh or cry, I skipped after him.

When we reached the entrance to the cabin, Dak turned and raised his hand to stop me. "You stay here; I'll go in first."

I nodded, accepting his reflexive gallantry.

He returned after a couple of minutes. "It's empty, but the door in the front is open."

I entered the cabin and looked around. "I must have left it open," I said, closing the French door. "I did rush out."

"Then it's okay?" Dak said.

"I guess. It's unlikely whoever came here would have lain in wait all night." Or had it all been my imagination? "Look, why don't we have a cup of coffee. I could use another one."

Dak and I had just sat down to drink our coffee when a vehicle drove up to the house.

"I'll go see," Dak said. He picked up the stick, which he had left in the entrance, and opened the door. "It's okay; it's just Jean-Marie."

Jean-Marie entered without a greeting. Despite the chill, he wore no sweater or jacket, only a white T-shirt, and the dark hair on his forearms was fluffed up against the chill.

"Hey, Jean-Marie, you look cold. How about some coffee?" I rose to get him a cup.

Jean-Marie looked around, his eyes wide and unfocused.

"What's up?" I said. "Is something wrong?"

Jean-Marie turned to me and blinked. "Yes," he said, "there is a dead man in the vineyard."

Chapter 9

"It was the vultures," Jean-Marie said.

The last word was muffled by the ivory cable-knit sweater he was pulling over his head. I had insisted he wear it despite his protestations that he would get it dirty.

"The what?" Dak said.

"The turkey vultures. I see some flying in a circle." Jean-Marie made the motion with his finger. "I thought maybe it was a deer somehow came through the fence and died, so I went to see." He swallowed. "It was not a deer. The vultures, they had started. I put my sweater on his head."

We stood in shocked silence for a moment. "Show us where," I said, heading to the door.

"Do you think it's the guy who was after you?" Dak said as we hurried down the driveway.

Jean-Marie grabbed my arm. "What is this?"

We all stopped.

"Someone came here last night. Clare had to stay with me," Dak said.

Jean-Marie sniffed. "Ah, yes, I can see." I had, I realized, absorbed the resin and wood smoke smell from Dak's hut. "What does it mean, someone is after you?" he continued.

I pulled out of his grasp. "It's a long story. I think we should go and see the body you found."

Jean-Marie led us down the drive to the bottom of the cliff, then around its base. Below the part of the cliff that projected out like the bow of a ship, some turkey vultures were hunched silently here and there on the fallen boulders.

"It is there," Jean-Marie said pointing.

The vultures watched our approach with baleful eyes, and when we were almost upon them they spread their wings and lazily lifted into the air only to settle down again just out of reach. We hadn't been able to see anything to that point, and it was soon apparent why. The body was lodged among the boulders upon which it had fallen, its limbs at unnatural angles, and the clothing, including Jean-Marie's sweater, which shielded the head, were all in neutral colours. I drew in a sharp breath. The jacket the body wore was made of charcoal grey leather.

"I think I know who it is," I said.

Jean-Marie glanced at me. "Do you still want to see the face?"

"Yes. Yes, I should."

"It is not very nice."

"I have to see."

Jean-Marie nodded and reached over to lift the sweater. The man's hair was blond and short-cropped, as I had expected, but the vultures had ravaged the man's eyes and the soft tissue of his face. My hand flew to my mouth, and I jerked back with a cry. Dak gagged but held it in. After the few moments it took for us to collect ourselves, we huddled together in a small circle of rocks.

"I think I heard it happen. There was a cry when I was running away from the cabin." I shivered, remembering. "I thought it was a bird."

"How do you know this man, and why he is here?" Jean-Marie said.

I gave him and Dak an abbreviated version of my encounter with Nick Duvall. When I spoke of his death, Dak sat up straighter and Jean-Marie swore, at least I think he did, in French. I concluded by describing my encounter with the dead man in my neighbourhood and at my condo, and then the experience of the previous night: the sound of someone approaching on foot, my flight, taking shelter with Dak.

"Did you tell the police about this man?" Jean-Marie said.

"Well, yes, but it's complicated," I said. "The ones in Vancouver had me down as one of their suspects for Duvall's murder, and I'm not sure I've completely convinced them that I'm innocent or that someone is following me."

"Maybe they will believe you now," Jean-Marie said, "or maybe they will think that it was you who killed this man."

I sat bolt upright. "But I didn't! I ran away; I was with Dak."

Dak nodded his head vigorously.

Jean-Marie glanced at Dak. "We can take away the body. I know some places where no one will find it. Or maybe into the ocean. Then the police will not know."

Dak and I stared, open-mouthed, at Jean-Marie.

"I … no, that's just wrong," I said. "It was clearly an accident. Did you see the guy's shoes? They're thin-soled, slippery, city shoes. He probably heard me leave and came after me. I went around to the side and followed the fence down, but he wouldn't have known that and probably went straight, toward the cliff edge. It was really dark last night, so he wouldn't have been able to see well, especially right after coming out of a lit room. The ground's uneven, and the grass is pretty slippery out there, so he wouldn't have had much traction. He probably slipped, lost his balance, fell over. The police will see that, surely. And we should call them soon."

I pushed myself up and dusted off the seat of my jeans. Dak followed with alacrity, his relief at not being party to the disposal of a body evident.

Jean-Marie rose more slowly. "If that is what you want. But it does not always go so well with the police."

"I certainly know that, but I don't think I have a choice."

"Okay," Jean-Marie said. "Dak maybe will stay to keep away the birds?"

Dak gave the crumpled figure a sidelong glance but nodded. "Yes, I can stay."

***

The local police force consisted of an outpost of the Royal Canadian Mounted Police. The constable who responded to my call looked like he still wasn't shaving daily, but he carried himself with authority and when taken to view the body eyed it with some relish. He took some preliminary statements from us, which extended only to my fleeing from an apparent intruder and then Jean-Marie's finding the body in the morning. He eyed us speculatively when we claimed not to know the man, catching, perhaps, the small hesitation on my part. Well, I *didn't* know him, did I?

The officer advised us with some regret that he would have to hand the case up the line. After spending some time on his cell phone out of earshot, he informed us that a more senior officer would join us soon, and a scene of crime squad from the Victoria headquarters would be coming over on the next ferry.

"Scene of crime?" I said, alarmed.

"The death *is* unexplained," the constable said coolly.

I started to say that it was obvious the man stumbled over the edge of the cliff in the dark but shut up when I thought it might suggest that I knew more about what happened than I did.

The investigative machinery rolled out over the course of the day. I wasn't allowed to go back to the cabin while the investigators poked around it and the area around the cliff where the guy had gone over, and Dak, Jean-Marie, and I were each drawn off to separate police cars where we waited to be questioned. This was done by the constable's superior, a dark, pale, bean-thin sergeant. The narrow gaze he levelled on me during my account made it clear that he didn't buy my story about not knowing the man who I claimed had been stalking me.

"Call Inspector Yuen at the Vancouver police," I said. "He knows all about it."

The sergeant hesitated, then nodded to the constable who had been taking notes.

We were released late in the afternoon, and I was given permission to return to the cabin.

"I can't stay there," I said to Jean-Marie.

"You are very welcome to come to stay with Jasmine and me," Jean-Marie said.

I doubted that Jasmine would have welcomed the impromptu invitation, and the notion of staying with her and Jean-Marie for any period of time boggled my mind, so I expressed my gratitude at his offer and declined.

"I'll call Kate to see if she has a room available," I said.

***

"Clare, hon, thank the Lord you're okay," Kate said. "When we saw all the commotion, I went to your gate but they wouldn't let me through. They said someone had died, and they wouldn't say who it was. We were so worried. Please say it's not Jean-Marie or Dak."

"No, it was a stranger, not anyone you'd know."

"What the heck was he doing to get himself killed, and why at your place?"

I sighed. "It's a long story. Kate, I need a room, maybe for a few days. Can you put me up?"

Kate said I'd be welcome to stay, so I packed my few things quickly and left. Outside the cabin, the place spoke only of peace. A light southeasterly soughed through the trees, the air was redolent with the wholesome smell of wet earth, and purple and gold crocus blooms studded the turf, impossibly lush and green from the spring rains. I started for my car but stopped before opening the door. I didn't want to have to drive through the throng of onlookers who had gathered at the gate over the course of the afternoon. I threw my suitcase over the deer fence and, fitting my toes into the wire web, hauled myself up and over to the other side.

Kate and Hugh's property did not extend the full length of mine, and the first section was forested. I found a narrow deer path and followed it to the gate in the wooden fence enclosing their backyard. I knocked on the kitchen door, startling Kate, who was busy at the stove.

"Clare, hon, come on in," Kate said, opening the door. She glanced over my shoulder at the yard.

"Sorry for the unconventional entrance," I said. "I'm avoiding the crowd."

"Yeah, there sure are a lot of folks out there," Kate said. "Vultures."

I swallowed hard at the word, remembering the dead man's face. "Can I sit down?" I said, suddenly exhausted.

"Oh, hon, of course. You're white as a ghost. Let me get some coffee on." She moved over to the coffee maker and called out, "Hugh, darling, Clare's here."

Hugh wheeled himself to the table where I sat with my head in my hands. Over steaming cups of coffee spiked with scotch and thick slices of carrot cake, I told them all that had happened since the previous night.

"You should have called or come here," Hugh interrupted when I mentioned staying with Dak.

"I didn't have time to phone, and I couldn't risk crossing paths with whoever was there."

My account of finding the dead man shocked them into silence. "It was the same guy who had been following me in Vancouver."

"Whatever did he want with you?" Hugh said.

"I haven't the slightest idea."

"And how the hell did he know you were here?"

"Yeah, I've been wondering about that too. He must have seen me when I went back to the condo for clothes the other day. I thought I had been careful, but he could have been hidden somewhere, watching for my return. Then he could have followed me to the ferry, may even have been on the same boat as me."

"Well, whatever the reason he was following you, it's probably all over now with him gone," Kate said, eminently practical.

"I hope so."

***

Kate took me up to my room, an airy space with a dormer window overlooking the woods at the back. The cherrywood furniture was traditional, the walls painted a soothing blue-grey. I longed to crawl under the voluminous duvet that smothered the bed but figured a shower and a change of clothes were needed first.

"You can stay in here until Friday when our next guests come, then we'll put you in Everett's room for the weekend," Kate said, referring to Hugh's adolescent son who lived with his mother in Calgary and visited monthly. She brushed aside the matter of payment, saying that they didn't charge their friends, but I insisted and we settled on a reasonable daily rate for my stay.

The next morning, a reporter from the island weekly newspaper came calling on Kate and Hugh, looking for their take on the death next door. Kate sent him off with a few choice phrases.

When the doorbell rang again, we assumed he had returned, but it was the RCMP constable to collect me for another round with his sergeant. During the silent ride to the town centre, I swayed from side to side in my seat as the constable took the curves in the road like a race car driver. At the RCMP's office, he left me to wait in a small chairless lobby for a few minutes, then he escorted me through the door and down a corridor to an office.

The face that looked out at me from the office was that of Inspector Yuen, and I hesitated with surprise in the doorway. He was slouched in a visitor's chair across the desk from the thin, dark-haired sergeant who had quizzed me the previous day. The sergeant waved me to the only other chair in the room. Neither man rose as I came forward and sat down. The air was dense with their maleness, and without thinking, I waved my hand before my face to clear it.

Inspector Yuen pushed himself up in his chair. "So, Clare, another dead body. That makes three now, huh?"

"It's the guy I told you about, the one who had been following me. I described him, remember?"

"Oh, yeah, I remember. So what happened? How did he go over that cliff?"

"I don't exactly know. I ran off when I heard him coming."

The sergeant leaned forward, stretched his arms out on his desk, hands clasped. "I thought you said in your statement yesterday that you didn't know who was approaching your house."

"That's right, I didn't then. I realized who it was when I saw him, his body, yesterday."

"If you didn't know who it was, why did you assume that the person wasn't friendly?" the sergeant continued. "It could have been your neighbour, or that guy living on your property, the one you spent the night with."

I winced at his phrasing. "It was late. I was all by myself."

"Still, it's a pretty odd reaction."

I swallowed, my throat suddenly very dry. "Strange things have been happening to me, so I was spooked." I glanced at Yuen for support. "Like I've told the inspector before. It didn't feel right, so I left."

The sergeant leaned back and studied me with narrowed eyes. "Here's what I think: Let's say this guy *has* been following you, he came to the door, maybe threatened you. You were scared; you had to get rid of him. You drew him outside, got him to follow you to the edge of the cliff, somehow got him to go over. Maybe you even gave him a little push."

I stared at him, my mouth opening and closing like a fish. "No! It wasn't like that at all. I *didn't* see who it was, because I got the heck out of the cabin before he arrived and I had absolutely nothing to do with his falling."

"It's perfectly understandable, if you felt threatened. It would be self-defense." The sergeant's voice was even, reasonable.

I was almost ready to believe him. I remembered what Jean-Marie had said about the police thinking I might be responsible. I wondered if we wouldn't have been better to dispose of the body as he had suggested. It occurred to me that I was quickly getting out of my depth, that maybe it was time to ask for a lawyer.

"No, look, I went around the side of the house and down the hill along the fence," I said, trying to keep my voice steady. "The guy probably heard me leave but went looking for me in the front, and it was so dark he wouldn't have seen the edge of the cliff. Dak, the fellow I stayed with, can vouch for me."

The sergeant raised a thin black eyebrow. "You could have pushed the guy over the cliff and then gone to Dak so he could give you an alibi. Or maybe he even helped you."

"No, it wasn't like that at all." I had a sudden thought. "Didn't your people go over the area at the edge of the cliff? The grass is pretty long out there, and if I had been tramping around like you say, my footprints would be all over."

I mentally crossed my fingers, hoping that the guy had in fact been alone when he fell. Yuen and the sergeant exchanged quick glances, and my heart leapt.

"There aren't any footprints, are there?" I said.

The sergeant cleared his throat. "What we may or may not have found out there is not your concern." His tone was stern, but I sensed a lack of conviction.

"Look," I said, addressing Inspector Yuen. Illogically, I considered him an ally. "I was not responsible for that man's death, and I think you know it. I don't even know who he is. Have you been able to find out?"

93

Yuen smiled faintly at me. He cocked his head in the sergeant's direction. "They found a car up one of the side roads near your place that they figure belonged to him. His name is Valerian Melnikov. My sources say he's part of the local Russian mafia."

I gaped at him. "Russian mafia! What on earth would the Russian mafia want with me?"

"Something pretty serious. He was packing," Yuen said.

It took me a moment to understand what he meant. "Oh," I said in a very small voice.

"We figure this Valerian guy may give us a new angle on Nick's Duvall's murder. That's why I'm here. And to see if you had anything more to say. You don't happen to have any other gems to share with us that might shed some light on the connection between these three dead guys, do you?"

I shook my head.

Yuen leaned towards me over the arm of his chair. "Like I said before, I think it all comes back to your boyfriend. I figure he was involved in something that got him killed—drugs, prostitutes, guns, whatever—and now it's blowing back on you. Like, you could have something they want, or know something, whose value or significance you don't realize."

"No, it can't be."

"Because if you really didn't do this and don't know what's going on—"

"I didn't, and I don't!"

"Then how else do you explain people around you dropping dead like flies?"

The sergeant had been following our exchange, and his frown suggested that he wasn't happy with the direction the discussion was taking. He started to say something, but I cut him off.

"You were going to look into Leo's affairs, his finances," I said to Yuen. "If Leo was involved in any criminal activity, wouldn't it show up there? What have you found out?"

Yuen sat back, increased the distance between us. "We can't really disclose any of that."

"Come on, what you were poking around in is my concern as well, or it will be soon. I think I have a right to know."

"Well, I guess so," Yuen said after a moment. "We had a good look at Leo's financial dealings going back, I dunno, fifteen years or so, and everything *seems* to be above board."

"So no apparent links to Nick Duvall, or this Valerian guy, or the Russian mafia?"

"No, but you know, these guys are pros. They know how to cover their tracks."

"Maybe there's just nothing to cover."

Yuen shrugged.

"There's got to be something else that explains all that's happened," I said. "You must have found *something* out about Duvall. Didn't you say he was in prison? Maybe it was some unfinished business from his time there, someone taking advantage of the crowds and the lack of context to settle some old score. Maybe Duvall's the link to Valerian Melnikov and Leo has nothing to do with it at all."

"Yeah, well, maybe. Organized crime's got some pretty strong ties on the inside, and Duvall was in the system for almost twenty-five years. But then we're back to what he wanted with Leo."

"What was Duvall in prison for?" I said.

"He killed a prison guard; anyway, that's what kept him in for so long. They had to move him out west from that penitentiary. The original crime was an assault conviction when he was young, just eighteen, in Quebec. Place with a funny name, Chibo-something."

My heart did a little skip. "Chibougamau?"

"Yes, that's it." Yuen looked at me curiously. "You know the town?"

"I've heard of it. Like you say, curious name. So when was Duvall released?"

"Last December, early in the month, if I remember correctly."

December. After twenty-five years. And then he came looking for Leo. Fragments of a memory floated at the edge of my thoughts.

I glanced at the sergeant, who sat with his arms crossed, looking thunderous. I suspected that he was not happy about how Inspector Yuen had hijacked his interrogation. "Look, I've told you all I can about how Valerian Melnikov may have died. I'd like to go now, if that's okay."

The sergeant nodded, not looking at me.

I rose, said goodbye, and left.

***

Chibougamau. The town where Leo had grown up.

What I had begun to remember when Inspector Yuen was speaking of Duvall was how distracted Leo had been as we were dressing for the party. *Something has come up,* he had said, *something from long ago.* It wasn't too big a stretch to surmise that what had come up involved Nick Duvall.

Up until this point, I had viewed the mysterious occurrences of the past three months—the car crash; Nick Duvall's calls, theft, and murder; Valerian Melnikov's stalking me, then his death—with a sort of detachment. Yes, I was in the middle of all the events, but incidentally, like a stone in a stream over and around which the water flows. The evidence of a concrete, undeniable link between Leo and Nick Duvall changed that. He may not have been an innocent party in these events. His past actions and associations could have been what had cost him his life and put mine in jeopardy.

In a way that it hadn't been previously, the whole business now was personal, a matter between Leo and me. For this reason, I had not told Inspector Yuen about the Chibougamau connection even though I knew he would be furious if, probably when, he found out. With Leo dead, I didn't think it would serve any purpose to have the police start looking under the rocks of his past. But that didn't mean I wasn't going to.

Chapter 10

Hugh and Kate listened quietly, nodding in apparent agreement when I told them that I intended to travel to Chibougamau, and why.

"How's your French?" Hugh said. "I don't think they speak much English up there."

"It's as good or as bad as you'd expect from someone who got middling grades in high school."

"Why don't you take Jean-Marie along?" Kate said, and before I knew it, she had gone out and called over the fence to where he was working. Any irritation I felt at her presumption was offset by the obvious logic of the idea.

Jean-Marie came over a half hour later, unlaced his work boots at the back door, and padded over to the table in his grey and white work socks, the heel of one of them showing a skillful darn in bright red yarn.

"Is this because of the dead men?" Jean-Marie said bluntly when I had given him a summary explanation of my planned trip, leaning heavily on nostalgia as a reason for going.

"Well, maybe indirectly," I admitted. "Whatever is behind all that's going on seems to have its roots in Chibougamau. I thought I'd try to find out more about Leo and Nick's pasts and maybe get answers to some of the questions I have, and it sounds like I'll need a translator."

"Ah." Jean-Marie thought for a long moment. "I am happy to go with you, but you will have to talk to Jasmine."

"Of course."

"And maybe not to say that it is about the man who was killed when he was with you, or the one who fell from the cliff."

***

Jean-Marie arranged for me to come over and speak to Jasmine on the following evening. I dressed carefully for the visit in a pair of jeans and a long, loose white sweater. I thought it best to downplay my feminine charms, such as they were.

Jasmine and I talked at their kitchen table over a cup of herbal tea, while Jean-Marie was in the living room entertaining Mischa. "So why would you want to go to Chibougamau, of all places? In Quebec it's like the back of beyond," she said.

I took a sip of the tea and set it aside—it tasted like boiled hay. "It's where Leo grew up, and, I don't know, I thought it would be nice to visit his old hometown to get some closure on his death."

The explanation was in the most general sense true, but I blushed at the clumsy explanation.

Jasmine twirled a curl around her finger. "So this isn't a business trip?"

"Well, not in the sense that I'm going there to conduct business, but it is related to the vineyard." Like, if Leo's hidden cache of money ended up being linked to something criminal, there wouldn't be one.

"And why do you need Jean-Marie with you?"

"I don't speak French. I need someone with me who does."

"And you couldn't just hire someone there to translate for you?"

"Perhaps," I said. I kept my voice patient. "But it's a personal matter, and I'd prefer not to have to work through a stranger."

Jasmine took a sip of tea and studied me. "And for how long?"

"Five days or so. Two days to get there and back, and then, maybe, three in Chibougamau. It should be enough to find out what I want to know."

"You would, of course, cover all of Jean-Marie's expenses."

"Of course."

Jasmine studied me for a long moment, a slight smile playing on her lips. She was enjoying her power, wondering, perhaps, how far she could push it without jeopardizing Jean-Marie's interests. A cluster fly dropped onto the table on its back and spun around like a manic breakdancer, sawing the silence. My mother's instructions in etiquette did not extend to rules for dealing with flies on someone else's table, so I let it be.

"Yes," Jasmine finally said. "Yes, I suppose he can go."

***

Jean-Marie and I left for Chibougamau on the Monday of the next week with the intention of returning on the following Friday. Chibougamau had an airport, but there were only a few flights in and out each day. The nearest city was Chicoutimi, a three-hour drive away. I wasn't averse to a bit of sightseeing, so I booked plane tickets to Montreal with the plan to spend the night there, catch a morning connection to Chicoutimi, pick up a car, and drive on to Chibougamau.

There was a limited choice of vehicles to rent at the Chicoutimi airport. I had hoped for a sturdy four-wheel-drive SUV, but the best they could offer was a mid-sized silver Dodge van equipped, they assured me, with tires suitable for snow. Although it was now April and notionally spring, the travel websites I had consulted warned of the area's changeable weather. With Jean-Marie's help, I completed the French-language rental documents. The counter clerk handed Jean-Marie the keys and the forms and gave him directions to the agency's lot. When we located the van, we had an awkward moment: Who would drive? I extended my hand for the keys and sat down firmly in the driver's seat.

During the trip, I spoke about what I wanted to accomplish during the visit. My inquiries would focus on Leo, the explanation being that my visit was a kind of pilgrimage inspired by his death. I would ask people about his life there, his family, his friends, specifically Nick Duvall. Although it was over twenty-five years since Leo had left, Chibougamau was a small town, and I figured that somewhere among its seven-thousand-odd souls I would find someone who remembered him.

The police station was the obvious place to start, given Nick Duvall's criminal history, but I wanted to proceed with more subtlety and keep the focus on Leo. So the preliminary inquiries would be at institutions, like the school, which were likely to have historical information. I had telephoned the school's administrative office before we left but was not able to get beyond Qui? Quoi? I tried again with Jean-Marie's help, and we succeeded in arranging a meeting with the principal for early that afternoon. Beyond that, my plans were vague, and there was little more we could discuss.

We completed the remainder of the trip exchanging only the occasional remark about the passing landscape. The countryside we drove through had the spare grey-hued beauty of the north, low-sloping hills, tight, dark forests of seemingly stunted trees, and many, many lakes. The clouds rolled above us in an endless sky, and two hours into the trip they let loose a dispirited rain that continued for the remainder of the drive.

Chibougamau was not at all what I expected. I imagined it as a picture-postcard Quebec town with antique steep-roofed limestone buildings, winding streets, and charming churches. The frontier town that Jean-Marie and I eventually rolled into sat next to a large lake and among long hills that looked like a giant hand had pressed down and gently flattened them. It had a raw edge, the public buildings low and flat-fronted, seemingly freshly hewn. The early spring slush coloured everything in a monochrome wash.

I pulled up to the main hotel located in the heart of the downtown and cranked the Dodge into a diagonal parking spot in front. Getting out of the vehicle, I had the urge to tether it to a hitching post. The hotel was a sprawling, two-storey affair with a modest lobby and a busy coffee shop. We were given rooms on the second floor, mine close to the elevator, Jean-Marie's three doors farther down.

Our appointment at the school was at two o'clock, and as it was already after one, we settled for a hurried sandwich lunch at the hotel café. With directions from the hotel clerk and a town map rimmed with ads for local businesses, we set out to find the high school. Nothing was very far away, and we reached it in four minutes, early for our meeting.

At the school, the principal's secretary, a prettily plump blond woman in her late thirties, told Jean-Marie that the principal was out on the playing field with his physical education class and would be in shortly. Jean-Marie translated my explanation that we were looking for information about Leo. Over the next few minutes, the secretary protested over and over that they could not release student records or other personal information and Jean-Marie assured her that this was not what we were after.

This might have continued indefinitely if the principal had not arrived. He sauntered in with bowlegged nonchalance, tossing a soccer ball from hand to hand. In his forties, he was apparently trying to hold middle age at bay with flat black hair dye and vigorous exercise. He was one long sinew, a fact underlined by the skin-tight clothing he wore. His athletic tights were positively sculptural. I had to struggle not to stare and didn't dare meet Jean-Marie's eyes.

The principal set a ball on his secretary's desk and listened to her explanation of our query with his hands on his hips. When she was done, he turned to us and repeated the business about not releasing student records and added that he was not at the school during the time in question.

"Ask him if he can refer us to someone who taught here twenty-five years ago and may have known Leo," I said to Jean-Marie. "Surely there is someone still around."

Jean-Marie conveyed the request. Discussion ensued between the principal and his secretary.

"The principal, he is here only nine years, and the secretary only four so they cannot think of anyone right away," Jean-Marie said. "Everyone who was here then is gone."

My heart sank. Had we hit a dead end so soon? Where would I go next?

The principal suddenly snapped his fingers. Jean-Marie listened, nodded, and translated. "He says that there is a lady who was teaching English when he first came and who he thinks was here for a long time. She is retired for many years."

Jean-Marie spoke to the principal, who nodded and said something to his secretary.

"They will telephone to this lady to see if she will talk to us," Jean-Marie said.

The secretary placed the call and after a brief conversation put her hand over the mouthpiece and spoke.

"Ah," Jean-Marie said, "this lady, Madame Edna McCrae, is happy to talk to us, and if we want we can go to her house now."

"Yes, yes, that would be great," I said.

The secretary completed the call with Mrs. McCrae and wrote out her address for us. We thanked her and the principal, and left.

***

Edna McCrae lived in one of the more impressive residences in Chibougamau, a two-storey brick house set back in a large yard. We pushed through the front gate and followed a curved walk edged with well-tended beds to the front door.

Edna had been waiting for us and opened the door as we approached. She was a small, tidy woman in her early seventies with close-cropped white hair and chic glasses in square black metal frames. She wore jeans with a neat crease and a white T-shirt under a pale peach cardigan. A round medallion of carved bluish rock suspended on a long leather cord hung around her neck.

"Hello!" she said.

Jean-Marie and I returned the greeting and shook her hand. She ushered us into her living room, a place with the formality of a display in a furniture store. We sat down on a pale blue brocade sofa suite set at right angles on a large blue, yellow, and green floral-patterned rug. A tray with both a coffee and a tea service and a plate of cookies sat at one end of a walnut coffee table.

Edna asked us what we would like and poured out the cups of black coffee we both requested.

"Sorry, they are store-bought. I don't bake," she said, presenting the plate of cookies.

Jean-Marie and I each took one to show that we didn't mind.

When she had poured out her own cup of tea and stirred in milk and a spoonful of sugar, Edna leaned back in her chair and said, "So what can I do for you?"

I repeated my line about Leo's death and my desire to know more about his early life.

Edna nodded. "Yes, I remember Leo, although he was known by his full name then. Like the painter, I once said to him." She sipped from her cup. "A big boy. Hard to miss. Quite bright, as I recall."

She set her cup and saucer down on the table and folded her hands on her lap. "The English class was optional then, and only in high school. Leonardo was very keen. He had already taught himself to read, so the first year was a bit tedious for him. I remember because he always tried to take the lesson further. The school didn't have a language lab at that time, so I brought in some of my own language tapes with a small recorder and let him work on them by himself in the spare room during class. I think he understood that knowing English would be the key to getting out of here. So many of the young people didn't go beyond high school. Many of the boys immediately went to work in the mines and married local girls, often when they were still very young." She shook her head.

"Did you know his parents?" I said.

"No. If there was any dealing with them, it would have been the homeroom teacher who did it."

"So his parents were still alive when he was in high school?"

"Well, yes, I think so. Or maybe ..." Edna frowned, concentrating. "I vaguely remember that there was something about the family." After a long moment, she shook her head. "Sorry, there was something, but I just can't recall."

"Can you suggest anyone else who may have known them?" I said.

Edna studied me for a moment, thinking. "Yes, Georges Seguin. He was the gym teacher at the time. Left a few years later to take over his father's business, something to do with construction. But he coached the different sports teams and knew most of the boys. My late husband liked to go to the hockey games, and I recall him saying once that one of the Barsoni boys was quite good." She smiled. "Not my cup of tea, though."

My heart did a quickstep. "Leo had brothers?"

Edna nodded. "One, yes, Mario. Older than Leonardo, but not by much. A year or two, perhaps. I never taught him, though." She sat forward. "That was it! That was what I was trying to remember. Mario died. He had already left school but was still quite young."

Edna wasn't able to remember the circumstances of Mario's death. "Georges may know better," she said.

When I asked her for Georges' telephone number, she offered to call him on my behalf.

Jean-Marie and I got up and followed Edna to the kitchen, where she placed the call. The kitchen had the same unused quality as the living room, but a sunroom running along its back was evidently where Edna spent her time. To one side sat an easel and a long table littered with an artist's paraphernalia—sheets of blank textured paper, brushes upended in mason jars, little discs of colour, scissors, rags. A pale green smock was draped over the back of a chair. I stepped through the doorway and down two steps into the sunroom for a better look. The windows gave a view to the lake on whose shore Chibougamau sat. Shafts of light cut diagonally through humps of cumulus, creating shifting patches of brightness on the lake's surface.

"How about tomorrow morning around ten?" Edna called from the kitchen.

"That would be great." I pulled myself away from the view and returned to the kitchen.

Edna completed the call and scribbled down some information. "Here's Georges' address," she said, handing me a piece of paper. She walked us to the door. I expressed our thanks for the coffee and the information, and we left.

***

On the way to see Georges Seguin the next day, I stopped at a drugstore, bought a lined notebook and some pens, and tucked the lot in my shoulder bag. I had overlooked the need to record the information we would receive—a measure of the distance I had come in the few months since I had last worked.

Georges Seguin lived in one of the residential neighbourhoods of Chibougamau on a street bare of trees. His house was a newer split-level rancher finished with beige vinyl siding. A straight concrete walk dissected the front lawn, connecting the sidewalk to a porchless entrance.

As we waited at the door for someone to answer our knock, I said, "Georges may not speak English. If you have to, do you know what to say by way of introduction?"

Jean-Marie nodded. The door opened.

"Mr. Seguin?" I said.

Georges Seguin replied in French, and Jean-Marie introduced us.

Seguin was around sixty and of medium height but powerful build. His receding sandy-grey hair curled on his collar. He invited us in with what sounded like an apology, his French flattened by a hard twang.

Jean-Marie turned to me. "Georges says that he hopes we do not mind, he is taking care of his granddaughter Caroline. His wife and daughter have gone shopping."

105

In the family room to which Georges led us at the back of the house we met Caroline surrounded by a collection of long skinny dolls with pink plastic skin and shanks of coarse hair. In response to a few words from Georges, she looked up and said bonjour.

Having recently had breakfast, we declined Georges' offer of coffee and sat down on a hard brown and green plaid sofa whose edges hung in shreds. The perpetrator sprawled on a small sheepskin pad near a woodstove, a paw over its eyes. I pulled the notebook and a pen from my shoulder bag.

Jean-Marie and Georges spoke for a few minutes. Jean-Marie turned to me. "Georges has a business to put up the walls in the new houses. Now it is the husband of his daughter who does the work."

I left them to their ice-breaking chatter. Jean-Marie mentioned first Leo's name, then Mario's. Georges replied at length. I had tuned out but caught Jean-Marie's glance when Georges mentioned Nick Duvall's name.

When Georges had finished, Jean-Marie turned to me and summarized. "Georges was the teacher to Leo and his brother, Mario, and they also played the hockey. He says Leo was maybe a little slow."

Georges interrupted briefly; he apparently understood some English.

Jean-Marie nodded his head and continued. "Georges put Leo as the goalie, and that was better."

I sympathized with the adolescent Leo, big and probably clumsy, as I had been at that age.

"Mario was good, Georges says, but the star was Nick Duvall. Georges thinks that Nick was maybe good enough for the NHL. He had much hope for Nick."

Georges spoke again. I glanced at Caroline and her dolls. She had been dressing them in tiny outfits and impossibly small moulded plastic high heels. Now she held a doll in each hand and in a chirping voice conducted what appeared to be a dialogue between the two.

After a few minutes, Jean-Marie spoke. "With Nick, the team was the champion, but Nick had a very bad temper." Georges put his finger pistol-like to his right temple and twisted his hand. He spoke, illustrating his words by cupping his hand and making a wrenching movement.

Jean-Marie raised his eyebrows and turned to me. "Nick was maybe even a bit crazy. One time, he had a fight and broke the arm of the other boy. Georges had to put Nick off the team."

Georges elaborated, chopping the air with his hand. Jean-Marie continued. "After Georges did that, someone cut the tires of his truck. He thinks Nick did it. There was no one else with a reason."

"What happened to all of them, Leo, Mario, and Nick? Does Georges know?" I said.

Jean-Marie translated, and Georges spoke at length. I caught movement out of the corner of my eye and turned to watch Caroline engaged in what appeared to be a fight between two of her dolls. She banged their heads together and ground the little plastic bodies against each other, all the while making low guttural sounds. The blond doll fell to the ground, and the one with sooty black hair danced over her in victory.

Jean-Marie touched my arm, and I turned to him. "Georges did not see the boys after they left school. Mario died, he thinks maybe in a fight. Nick beat up some man and went to jail. Georges was not surprised. He does not know what happened to Leo."

"Ask Georges if he can suggest anyone else who can tell us more about what happened to them," I said.

Jean-Marie complied, and Georges thought for a moment before speaking. "Luc Brossard," Jean-Marie translated. "He was the police here for a long time. Georges says Luc knows everything."

"Would he know how we can contact him?" I said.

Jean-Marie said something, and Georges nodded. He drew the telephone, which sat on a side table, forward and pulled a slender telephone book out from a magazine rack. After consulting the book, Georges punched in a number and talked for a few minutes, mentioning Nick's, Mario's, and Leo's names. He hung up and spoke to Jean-Marie.

Jean-Marie nodded and turned to me. "This man, Luc Brossard, he will talk to us at two o'clock. There is a bar ..." Jean-Marie consulted briefly with Georges. "It is downtown." He named the cross street.

There being little more to be said, we thanked Georges and prepared to leave. I was putting the cap on my pen when Georges spoke. Jean-Marie's eyebrows rose at what he said.

"What is it?" I said.

"Georges says it is funny that we talk about Nick. He saw Nick here in the town in the winter."

"Does he remember when exactly it was?" I said.

After a brief exchange, Jean-Marie said, "He says February, because it was for a few days warm then, and the snow, it was melting in the street."

That meant Duvall visited Chibougamau in the time between his two telephone calls to me, his trip probably financed by the sale of Leo's stereo equipment. I uncapped my pen and wrote in my notebook: Why did Nick Duvall return to Chibougamau after all this time? What was he looking for?

Chapter 11

Jean-Marie and I arrived a few minutes early for our meeting with Luc Brossard. Inside the door to the bar, we stopped to let our eyes adjust to the gloom. The smell of stale smoke and spilled beer tinged with pine-scented cleaner greeted us. A bulky figure detached itself from a collection of dim shapes and stepped forward.

"You're the ones who want to talk?" Luc Brossard said. His English was accented but easy.

We shook Luc's hand and introduced ourselves. Luc gestured us towards a scarred wooden table near the main counter and pulled out a chair for me. Jean-Marie sat down to my right, and Luc in the chair across. I set my bag down on the empty seat on the left and drew out my pen and notebook. The barman sauntered up to us and took a swipe at the tabletop with a striped cloth. He was tall and blond, and his carefully cut hair, black designer jeans, and blue oxford shirt struck an incongruous note in the tired saloon. We all ordered the draft beer, a pint for Luc and glasses for Jean-Marie and me.

While we waited for the drinks, I looked around the room. There were only two other people there: a couple with their heads together in a far corner. Not surprising, given the hour of the day.

I turned back to my companions, who were exchanging pleasantries in a mix of English and French. "You speak English well," I said to Luc.

Luc nodded. "My mother was an Anglo. I come from Montreal. I was a cop there, and I got shot." He tapped his left shoulder. "It scared my wife. She grew up in Chibougamau and said we should come back here to live so our kids—they were just babies—could grow up to know their father." He shrugged. "It seemed like a good idea at the time."

The bartender brought the beers, and Luc emptied half of his pint in one long draught. He drank like he needed to, but I didn't make the mistake of thinking him a lush. He had the watchfulness and collected energy of a predator. Deep pouches cushioned cynical eyes, and sharp lines bracketed a hard mouth. His silver-streaked hair had receded at his temples to form a pronounced widow's peak. Luc mentioned having retired the previous year, and the restlessness with which he shifted in his seat and played with a pack of cigarettes on the table suggested that he hadn't yet adjusted to his new life. He selected a cigarette from the pack and tucked it in the corner of his mouth, then immediately took it out.

"Will you permit?" he said, holding the cigarette up.

"Go ahead."

Luc lit the cigarette and sucked on it hard. He exhaled a stream of smoke over his shoulder, coughed, and said, "So you're looking for Nick Duvall."

Jean-Marie and I exchanged glances. "Actually," I said, "I'm trying to find out about Leo Barsoni. He was my fiancé, and he was killed in a car accident last December. Nick comes into it only because he's the one who got me interested in Leo's past here in Chibougamau. Nick had, uh, recently been in touch with Leo, kind of out of nowhere. Then Nick called me after Leo died. But Nick also died before I had a chance to talk to him." I hoped my jumbled explanation had made sense.

Luc had lifted the pint to his mouth. He put it back down. "Nick is dead?"

"Yes. I understand he was here not long ago."

"Yes, he was." Luc laced his fingers across his stomach and studied me closely, his drink forgotten. "What happened to Nick?"

I hesitated. "He was killed, stabbed."

Luc's eyebrows shot up. "Stabbed? Where?"

"In Vancouver."

"What was he doing there?"

"I don't really know, only that he had contacted Leo."

"So who did it?"

"The police don't know."

"Huh!" Luc continued to stare at me as he chewed on this news. Then he shook his head. "But it was never Nick and Leo. It was the other brother, Mario, who was Nick's friend. What did Nick want with Leo, and after all this time?"

I had to stop myself from blurting out the whole story about my two conversations with Nick and the horror of our meeting. Luc had that effect; he must have been an effective interrogator. "That's just it," I said, "I don't know. It's partly why I'm here. But I also want to see where Leo came from, find out what his life was like here, growing up."

Luc released me from his scrutiny and drank some beer. The effect was almost physical. I sagged back in my chair, shakily picked up my glass, and took a sip.

Luc set his pint down on the table, took a last draw on his cigarette, and then stubbed it out in an ashtray. "So what do you want from me?"

"I'd like you to tell me what you can about Leo and his family."

Luc shook his head. "Leo I didn't know, just to recognize. A big kid. Stayed out of trouble. That's about it."

"Tell me about Mario, then. He died, didn't he?"

"Didn't Leo tell you?"

"He didn't say much," I said. All Leo had ever told me was that he had no family left. "Maybe it was still upsetting to him."

Luc nodded, more out of courtesy than conviction. "Mario wasn't a bad kid. Not what you would call a go-getter. Always after a good time. He and Nick, and there were three other guys, they hung around together. Thought a lot of themselves. Dressed really smart. Always seemed to have money to splash around." He shook his head. "Don't know where they got it. Some of them, okay, their parents weren't poor. Gerard Morgon, his dad was a foreman at the mine. Richard Proulx, his dad owned the pharmacy. Robert Fournier, his dad was a lawyer and the mayor."

I scribbled the names in my notebook.

"But Mario's family didn't have much, especially after the old man died," Luc continued, "and Nick's family was always poor. Seven kids, and his dad drank away whatever money he got. I suspected Nick was dealing drugs, small stuff. It would explain a lot, the money, why those rich kids who should have known better were friends with him. But I never could catch him."

"How did Mario die?" I said.

"He tried to stop a fight. He was considered something of a hero."

"What exactly happened?" I said, but Luc's gaze had lifted to a point above my head.

"*Ah, salut, Gilles!*"

The object of his greeting, a tall man with a gaunt face and thin white hair, tapped his way to the table with a cane. Luc stood up and dragged a chair from one of the other tables over next to his own and then helped Gilles out of his parka. I pulled the chair that held my bag back to make room. Gilles sat down with a grimace, the knobby knuckles of his hand white under papery skin as he leaned on the cane. His red and black lumberjack shirt looked slept in, and he gave off a fusty old-man odour. A widower, I figured.

Luc, still standing, asked Gilles something in French. He glanced at us. "Do you want another?" Neither Jean-Marie nor I had drunk much, and we shook our heads. Luc nodded at the barman, who had been following the exchange. The barman drew a couple of pints of beer and slid them across the counter. Luc set a pint in front of Gilles and one at his own place and then sat down. Gilles protested, and Luc calmed him with a motion of his hand.

"What's that all about?" I said, quietly, to Jean-Marie.

"Gilles wants only a small glass, but Luc said he will pay."

Luc introduced us to Gilles. "I hope you don't mind that he joins us."

I would have preferred that Luc wasn't distracted, but I said, "Not at all. Anyhow, you were saying about Mario ...?"

"Oh, yes." Luc took a quick sip of beer. "You know, I still remember that night. December 23, 1972. I had been in Chibougamau for just two years. It was usually pretty quiet here, not much happened. You could go for days without any real trouble. After Montreal, well, sometimes it was boring. But that night, it was like the town had gone crazy. There were only two of us on duty, and we had to call in the chief and the off-duty officers."

Luc started to shake a cigarette loose from his pack but changed his mind and pushed it aside. "First of all, a car had gone through the ice at the edge of the lake." He held up his left hand and bent the pinkie with the thumb and index finger of his right. "A kid had his dad's car, was showing off for his girlfriend. They got out just in time, but we didn't bring up the car until the spring.

"Then there were two fires." Each fire merited a finger. "One was deliberately set, some rags in a trash can behind the Jehovah's Witnesses' church. The other was in the movie theatre. Some Christmas decorations too close to a light bulb. Now that was scary. We had to evacuate the place.

"And old man Didier was mugged." Another finger. "He was the guy who owned the hardware store. Or maybe it was the next day. That was when they found him, anyway. And then Maurice Gervais, the plumber, ran his car into the back of a snowplow. Black ice, couldn't stop. No seat belt, of course, so he got pretty smashed up. There was just one ambulance, and it almost didn't get to him in time.

"Then those crazy Potvins, the four boys and the girl." With the last finger, Luc's hand had closed into a fist, and he opened it again and gazed at it speculatively, as though deciding how many digits to assign to the Potvins. He abandoned the count and continued. "They all came home for Christmas, got drunk, started an argument. One of them got hold of an old goose gun and started shooting. Two had to go to hospital, the other three I brought in, even the girl. She was the worst, yelling all the time."

Luc drew on his beer and wiped his mouth with the back of his hand. "On top of all that, Nick Duvall decides to pick a fight with the kid at the gas station. Nick was a testy guy, didn't take much to set him off. I don't know, maybe the kid looked at him the wrong way. Mario was with him, and Robert Fournier. Robert was at the university then, but he had come home for Christmas. Anyhow, Nick punched up the boy—I've forgotten his name—and the kid's dad, Jean Desjardins, he owned the gas station, he comes out from the back and tells Nick to lay off. But by this time, Nick has flipped and he goes after the old man.

"The Fournier boy called us from the garage, but by the time we arrived Nick had hurt the dad pretty bad, too. I took the three boys to the station, but with the racket the Potvins were making and everything else going on I just kept Nick in and sent Mario and Robert home. What I didn't know until after was that Mario had tried to break up the fight. Desjardins had a big wrench and was taking a swing at Nick, but Mario got in the way and took it in the stomach." Luc drew his hand across his midriff and said a few words to Gilles, who nodded in response.

"No one knew how badly Mario had been hurt, and he died the next day. Internal bleeding from a ruptured spleen. Desjardins felt really bad, but he was cleared at the inquest."

We sat in silence for a moment. I noticed the barman leaning against the counter nearby, following the discussion, polishing glasses with his striped cloth. The one he had used to wipe the tabletop. I glanced at my beer and decided I had had enough.

"What happened to them all after?" I said.

"Nick was charged with aggravated assault on both the kid and the dad. Because he was eighteen he got only a couple of years, but while he was in jail he roughed up one of the other detainees, pretty badly because he got another year or so inside. Again, he got into a fight with another inmate." Luc snorted. "Nick was a good-looking guy and probably attracted some unwanted attention. But when a guard tried to break it up, Nick turned on him and smashed him against a wall. It was cinderblock, and the guard hit his head hard and died, and that put Nick in for life, whatever that means nowadays."

"He got out last winter," I said. "He must have come back to see his family then."

Luc shook his head. "The Duvalls all left long ago." He spoke briefly with Gilles and nodded. "Gilles says they left in the mid-seventies."

"So what had he wanted here?"

Gilles spoke, and Luc listened attentively. They glanced at the barman, who was mixing a highball. He pushed the drink and a pint he had drawn to a customer and accepted a couple of bills in payment. When he had closed the cash register, Luc called him over and asked him a question. The barman shook his head.

"What's going on?" I said to Jean-Marie.

"Gilles said he saw Nick Duvall in this bar a few weeks ago and that he talked to the barman, but the barman said he can't remember everyone who comes in."

Luc said something that seemed to shock Gilles.

"Luc has just told Gilles that Nick was killed," Jean-Marie said.

"Sorry, we were just wondering who might have killed Nick," Luc said, turning back to us. "Not that he wasn't the sort to make enemies. And we're wondering what he was doing in Vancouver. For someone who was in jail so long, he seemed to have had business all over the country."

I could have told them what his business in Vancouver was about but didn't. "These other old friends of Nick's, the ones you mentioned earlier, are they still around?" I said. "Gerard, I think was one, and this Robert who was with them the night Mario was killed." I checked my notebook. "And then Richard Proulx."

Luc shook his head. "They all left. Gerard Morgon is in Chicoutimi, has a lumberyard there. You might be able to find him." I wrote the information down.

Gilles said something that made Luc laugh. "Gilles says that Nick got Gerard's sister pregnant, so he may not be too happy to talk to you about him.

"The Proulx dad sold up some time ago, and they moved away. The boy, Richard, he became a doctor, in Montreal, I think. He is probably in the phone book. And Robert Fournier ..." Luc grunted. "Our Monsieur Fournier is not only the local member of the national assembly, Quebec's legislature, but also the minister of finance."

I noted Fournier's position. "So I should be able to find his telephone number at the Quebec legislature."

"Well, you can try to talk to him, but good luck," Luc said. "He's a busy man."

I shrugged. "What happened to the Barsonis after Mario died?"

"Gilles knew them, I think," Luc said. He spoke briefly to Gilles, who replied at some length. When he finished, Luc nodded and turned to us. "Gilles worked with Paolo Barsoni in the mine. The Barsonis came, he thinks, in 1962 or '63. Paolo died a few years later, maybe 1971, he's not sure."

Gilles spoke again, punctuating his last words by swiping one dry palm hard against the other. Luc translated. "He said it was very sudden, some kind of cancer of the insides, and in just three months Paolo was gone."

I scribbled down the information. "So that left Leo, Mario, and their mother. Or were there other children?"

Luc conferred with Gilles and said, "No, there were just the two boys. After Paolo died, Gisela, the mother, had to get a job, cleaning at the mine's offices, Gilles says. Then when Mario died, she left. The other boy, Leo, too. They both left."

I asked Gilles if he knew where they had gone, and Luc translated. After a brief exchange, Luc said, "Gilles doesn't know where they went. He didn't know the family well, just Paolo, and he completely lost touch after Paolo died."

I looked at the dates I had written in my notebook. Leo would have been seventeen at the time of Mario's death, and he had started university in Vancouver in 1974. He and his mother had been somewhere for the intervening year. *Did Leo's mother come to Vancouver with him? Ask Karen,* I wrote. When we had spoken about Leo's will, Karen had made no mention of Leo's mother.

Addressing both Gilles and Luc, I said, "Do either of you know of anyone who was friends of the Barsonis and might be able to tell us more?"

Luc shook his head and translated the question for Gilles. "Gilles recalls Paolo talking about some neighbours named Godbout, how they had helped Paolo and Gisela when they first arrived. But he can't remember the first name."

"I wonder if they're still here?" I turned to the bartender, who once again was polishing glasses, and asked him if he had a copy of the telephone book for the town; he had been following our conversation and appeared to understand English. The bartender hesitated, then pulled the slim volume from a shelf beneath the cash register. I got up, took it from him, and brought it over to the table. When I found the page with the three Godbouts, I turned the book around for Luc and Gilles to see. Gilles tapped one of the names, Roger Godbout, and said something.

"That's the street where Paolo used to live. He says they used to be at number twenty-two," Luc translated.

I wrote down the address and telephone number and asked the bartender if we could use his phone for a local call. He eyed me warily and glanced at Luc, who said something. In response, the bartender handed a cordless handset over the counter.

"Would you mind?" I said to Jean-Marie.

He keyed in the Godbout's telephone number and, after a few minutes' conversation, punched the Off button. "They are happy to have us come at five o'clock," he said. He rose and returned the handset to the bartender.

I got up as well and extended my hand to Luc, then Gilles. "I can't thank you enough for your time. You've been very helpful." I placed a fifty-dollar bill in the centre of the table. "For the drinks." Jean-Marie and I said our goodbyes and turned to leave. As I slung the strap of my bag over my shoulder, I glanced back. Luc had slid the money over to Gilles and was drawing his own wallet out of his pocket.

***

We returned to the hotel for a brief rest before heading out to meet the Godbouts. When we arrived at their place, I walked past it to number twenty-two, three doors away, a small house with grey stucco siding that Gilles said had been the Barsoni home. A tricycle lay on its side on the dead grass, and other colourful children's toys lay scattered about. I had a hard time placing Leo in the setting but snapped a photo anyway, then returned to Jean-Marie who had been waiting for me by our van.

The Godbouts lived in a bungalow trimmed with barn-red siding. Mrs. Godbout, a chunky woman in her sixties with a halo of faded auburn frizz, was sweeping the front stoop when we arrived. She led us into the house, seated us in their living room, and called for her husband. A husky man with a pale brush cut, round red cheeks, and a gap between his teeth appeared briefly at the doorway waving a jug of wine. He and Mrs. Godbout had a brief exchange, and he disappeared.

"It seems we are to have Monsieur Godbout's wine," Jean-Marie said. His suspicions were born out when Mr. Godbout reappeared with the jug, now open, and a tray of tumblers. He sat down on the sofa next to his wife and started to fill the glasses. I declined, saying I had to drive, but something got lost in translation because I found myself accepting half a glass. I tried to give Jean-Marie a dirty look, but he refused to meet my eye. The wine smelled like a mixture of jam and sewer and tasted worse. I set mine aside after one sip.

Madeleine and Roger Godbout were jolly folk, laughing often as they reminisced about their friendship with the Barsonis. Jean-Marie translated in summary whenever they paused for breath. "The Barsonis lived down the street for maybe ten years. They were friends more with Monsieur Barsoni. Madame Barsoni spoke only a little French, and they say she was a bit proud."

Mr. Godbout rolled his eyes up and wiggled his head and shoulders in an *ooh la la* gesture, and his wife slapped him on the thigh.

"What's that about?" I said.

"It seems Leo's mother was nice to look at. Monsieur Godbout calls her 'Sophia Loren.'"

The Godbouts offered us more wine, which we declined, and refilled their own glasses. They spoke in a continuous stream, often finishing each other's sentences. Jean-Marie listened but didn't translate. I touched him on the arm. He nodded at the Godbouts and turned to me. "They talk about the Barsonis. They tried to grow tomatoes, and Monsieur Barsoni brought the grapes all the way from Montreal to make wine." Jean-Marie made little stamping movements with his feet. "He crush them in a washtub with his feet. That is how Monsieur Godbout learned to make wine."

"What do they remember about the boys?" I said.

Jean-Marie relayed the questions and, after a couple of minutes of conversation, turned back to me. "Leo, they say, was very quiet, very serious. Not like Mario. Mario was very handsome, they say, always friendly. After Monsieur Barsoni died, they did not see the family much. Monsieur Godbout tried to help Madame Barsoni, but she did not want it."

I could imagine what kind of help Monsieur Godbout had offered. "Ask them if they know what happened to Leo and his mother after Mario died."

Jean-Marie interrupted the Godbouts, who, now on their third glass of wine, were laughing uproariously at some memory. Mrs. Godbout answered. When she finished, Jean-Marie said, "Leo lived with one of his teachers until the school was finished, and then he went away, they do not know where."

"Just Leo? Where was his mother?"

Mrs. Godbout responded briefly, and Jean-Marie nodded. He turned to me. "After the funeral for Mario, Madame Barsoni went back to Sardinia."

***

We took our leave of the Godbouts shortly afterward, and, despite Jean-Marie's having valiantly finished his tumbler of wine, I handed him the keys to the Dodge and asked him to drive. I sat silent during the ride back to the hotel, in a mild state of shock. When I got to my room, I threw myself down on one of the beds, put my hands behind my neck, and stared at the ceiling.

Sardinia was a distinct part of Italy, yet Leo had never mentioned it being his home. Once, when we were planning a holiday, I had suggested that we go to Italy. I had never been there and assumed that, since it was Leo's homeland, he went back from time to time. Leo had said he had no interest in returning; he had severed his ties for good when he was eight years old. And, thinking back, Leo hadn't incorporated much of his native culture into his life. I remembered teasing him once about not liking pasta. "I grew up on it," he had said. "I had enough for a lifetime."

And then there was the matter of his mother. How could she have left him behind after Mario died? Why hadn't they stayed together, or at least in touch? Leo had said that he had no family. I had interpreted this as meaning they were all dead, but was it some kind of a metaphorical statement? Could his mother still be alive?

I sighed, swung my legs over the side of the bed, and sat up. The biggest question of all was why Leo had maintained such a strict secrecy about this part of his life. What did this say about our relationship? Would he ever have told me? I pulled my notebook from my bag and jotted down all the questions except for the last ones. I wasn't sure I would ever find the answer to them. Flipping to the first page, I reread all the notes I had taken that day, adding additional points I remembered. I finished with a to-do list. High on it was tracking down Nick and Mario's old friends. Even the one who was now the minister of finance. Especially the minister of finance. He had been there the night Mario had been fatally injured.

I glanced at the clock. Jean-Marie and I were to meet in the lobby at seven thirty to go out to dinner, and it was almost time. I put the notebook on the bedside table and went to the bathroom to freshen up. A touch of foundation and a lick of lipstick, and I was ready to face the world. I picked up my bag and left the room.

***

Jean-Marie and I went to a restaurant three blocks up from the hotel that claimed to offer regional cuisine. I ordered grilled northern pike, and Jean-Marie had venison brochettes. In between picking tiny forked fish bones out of my teeth, I laid out my plans for the next day.

"I wish I could find someone who had been Leo's friend. I'd like to talk to the teacher, the one with whom Leo lived until the end of the school year, maybe he would know. I forgot to ask his name— I'm assuming it was a he. Would you mind telephoning the Godbouts, maybe even tonight, to find out the teacher's name? Also, I'd like to follow up with the guys who were Nick and Mario's friends. Maybe we can track down their phone numbers tomorrow. We might be able to speak to the fellow in Chicoutimi, and possibly the doctor in Montreal, on our way back. How do you feel about staying one more day?"

Jean-Marie shrugged his shoulders. "I will ask Jasmine. She will call tonight."

We finished and sauntered back to the hotel, breathing the crisp evening air, and stopping to look into the lit shop windows we passed on the way. At my door I stopped and drew out my key. "In all, not a bad day. Eight thirty for breakfast tomorrow?" Jean-Marie agreed, said good night, and continued down the hall to his room. I turned my key in the lock, opened the door, and stepped into shambles.

Chapter 12

You know those dreams when you try to scream and nothing comes out? That's what happened when I stepped back into the hall to call Jean-Marie. Something must have caught his attention, because as he was unlocking his door he glanced back in my direction. I motioned to him, *Come, come!* He hesitated, then walked back towards me.

"Are you okay?" he said.

"Come and see," I said hoarsely, waving him into the room.

"Ah," said Jean-Marie.

The mattresses from the two beds were upended. The bedclothes had been torn off and lay in heaps on the floor. The armchair lay on its side, and the lamps, shorn of their shades, had been knocked to the ground. The drawers from the bedside tables had been yanked out, and their contents dumped on the floor. The book I had been reading lay face down in a corner, its pages curled under. My clothes had been pulled from the bureau drawers and closet hangers and cast about. I scooped up some underwear and stuffed it into my suitcase, which sat like a wide-open mouth in the midst of the mess. I continued to collect my clothes because it seemed better to do something than to stand and gape.

"What did these people want?" Jean-Marie said, righting the chair. "Do you have everything?"

I looked around. "I can't tell yet."

"We will arrange things, and then you can see," said Jean-Marie.

Together, we put the mattresses back into position and made up the beds, somewhat untidily, I confess, but I was too distracted to fold the corners sharply. While Jean-Marie saw to the lamps, I picked up the Gideon's bible and hotel brochures and stuffed them back in the drawers.

"My notebook!" I said. "The one I bought this morning. It was on the stand here. Do you see it anywhere?" I rechecked all the drawers and knelt down and looked under both beds. Jean-Marie went through the hall closet and stuck his head in the bathroom. "I do not see it."

"Why would anyone want my notebook?"

He studied me for a moment. "Maybe someone does not like the questions you are asking."

No, I thought, *someone definitely doesn't like that fact that I am here.*

"Do you want to call the police?"

I shook my head. "It's just a stolen notebook, and I've had enough of police."

Jean-Marie raised his eyebrows but let it go. "Then you will stay with me tonight."

"It's okay, I can get another room."

"Someone is not happy that you are here, and if they see something in your little book that they do not like, they will find you in another room."

"Well, they could find your room too."

"Yes," Jean-Marie said, "but I will be there."

***

If I hadn't been shaken by the events of the evening, I would have found the business of moving into Jean-Marie's room more awkward than I did. As it was, I merely nodded when he indicated that I should take the far bed and dropped my suitcase on the floor between it and the window. By then it was close to ten o'clock, and I began preparations to go to sleep. Jean-Marie suggested that I use the bathroom first. I gingerly moved his razor and toothbrush to the side and set my small overnight bag in a corner. After washing the day off my face and brushing my teeth, I changed into my nightgown. Fortunately, it was basically a long T-shirt and ran no risk of violating anyone's sense of modesty. When I was finished Jean-Marie took his turn, and as I crawled into bed I heard the rush of the shower. I opened my book, smoothed out the creased pages, and tried to read.

The shower had just been turned off when the telephone rang. I let it ring three times and had extended my hand to answer when Jean-Marie flew out of the bathroom, landed flat on his stomach on his bed, and snatched the receiver from its cradle.

"*Oui ... allô, chérie,*" he said breathlessly.

He was still wet from the shower, and all he wore was a towel around his waist, the edge of which lifted when he hit the bed to expose the curve of a taut white buttock. I sniggered, and Jean-Marie waved his hand angrily at me. Nodding, I clamped my hand across my mouth, but snorts continued to issue through my nose. I rose and hurried to the bathroom. I closed the door, sat down on the toilet, and gave myself over to uncontrollable hilarity. Desperate, I stuffed a washcloth into my mouth, but nothing could stop the laughter.

The murmur of Jean-Marie's voice ended, and he came to the door and knocked.

"Come on in," I called merrily. I had removed the washcloth from my mouth and was mopping my eyes.

Jean-Marie opened the door and glared at me. He clutched the towel closed at his waist.

"I can't help it," I giggled.

Jean-Marie yanked his clothes off the hook on the door. "Not that it matters so much now that you have seen me *sans culotte*," he said, and left the room. When he returned clad in his jeans and a white T-shirt, he was carrying a couple of small bottles of cheap brandy from the mini-bar. He cracked both open and dumped the contents into one of the toothbrush glasses. "Here," he said.

I hiccupped and shook my head.

"Drink it!"

"But I don't want it. I don't like brandy."

"You have the hysterics, and if you do not drink this I will have to slap you. I do not want to slap you."

"No." I bit my lips to try to contain the laughter. It was all so extraordinarily funny. I accepted the glass and took a big swig.

"Finish it!"

I shook my head but complied. A shudder convulsed my body, and a magnificent warmth flowered in my midriff. The laughter was gone.

"Now you should sleep."

I nodded meekly, rose and went to bed.

***

The brandy did its work, and I slept deeply without dreaming. When I woke, the clock read 7:34. I rubbed my eyes and glanced at the next bed. The coverlet had been removed, but the bed had not been slept in. I sat up and looked around. Jean-Marie was asleep in the armchair, which he had moved around to face the door. The coverlet was pulled up to his chin, and his head lolled against one side of the headrest. I got up and gently touched his shoulder. A hand shot out from under the cover and closed on my forearm like a vice grip. His eyes flashed open, hooded and feral, but they softened and his face relaxed when he saw me.

"Ah, Clare," he said, and loosened his hand.

"I'm sorry to wake you, but you looked so uncomfortable," I said, rubbing my forearm.

Jean-Marie slowly stood up and stretched. He still wore his jeans and T-shirt.

I picked the bedspread off the floor and began folding it. I motioned to the chair. "Why …?"

Jean-Marie scrubbed at his face. "In case the people who went to your room came back," he said through his fingers. "We will leave this morning."

I set the folded bedspread down and smoothed the top. "But there still are people I want to talk to. I've come all this way."

"Clare …"—Jean-Marie paused—"the ones last night, if they just want your book, they would not make the mess in the room." He shook his head. "It was not necessary, and it was violent. They are saying that they can be violent with you, too. There is something in this story of Leo and Mario and Nick we do not know yet, and someone wants to make sure that we do not find out. Maybe we have come too close and do not know it. I think of what happened to Nick, and I worry."

I remembered the dead weight of Nick Duvall's head in my hand, and my stomach knotted. I nodded.

Jean-Marie motioned to the bathroom. "Get ready, and we will go."

***

I showered and dressed. The previous night I had tossed the clothes that had been scattered around my room in my suitcase any which way, so I removed them all and repacked neatly. Jean-Marie paced the room waiting for me to finish. He protested when I suggested breakfast, but I said that it wouldn't take long and there wasn't really anywhere to have a meal along the way.

I swallowed some tart yoghurt and tasteless oatmeal. Jean-Marie gulped down three cups of coffee and some plain buttered toast.

When he finished, he rose abruptly. "I will put the valises in the car," he said.

I settled my account with the hotel and went out to where our Dodge van was parked. Jean-Marie stood by the driver's door jiggling the keys.

"Why don't I drive?" I said. "You didn't sleep much last night."

"I am okay. Let us go."

I navigated us through the streets with the aid of the town map, and we connected to the main highway heading south. We rode in silence, the town thinning around us. Jean-Marie's eyes flicked to the rear-view mirror from time to time. "What is it?" I finally said.

"I think someone is following us."

My head snapped around. "What? It's broad daylight."

"Use your side mirror. The green truck."

I twisted back to check my mirror. The truck, a dark green Ford, was the third vehicle behind and seemed to hover over the small black and beige cars between us. "But how can you tell?" I said. "They could just be in the line of traffic going in the same direction."

"It was parked down the street from the hotel this morning. It left when we did."

My stomach tightened. "What do we do?"

"Keep going. Maybe they just want to make sure that we leave." He swung out and passed the small red pickup ahead of us.

The Ford pulled out, passed the car in front, and settled back into our lane, restoring the two-car separation. I gasped. "Did you see that?"

Jean-Marie nodded, his mouth set in a hard line. "I think we are okay when there are still other cars."

We continued on in this manner for several miles, the line of cars moving as a unit. The black car turned into a driveway. The countryside was becoming wilder, only the occasional house now and fewer side roads. The red pickup turned off on one of them. Jean-Marie accelerated, and we started to pull away from the beige car that was now all that separated us from the Ford truck. Our pursuers, as it was now clear they were, veered into the passing lane and swung around the beige car. The space between us slowly shrunk.

"So that is how it is," Jean-Marie said. He glanced at me. "You have put on your seat belt?"

I nodded and gripped the armrest on my door. Jean-Marie pressed on the gas and our Dodge van surged forward, but the Ford kept pace and the space between us shortened.

"What are you going to do?" I said. My throat was so tight I could barely squeeze out the words.

"Try to get away."

Jean-Marie urged the van forward, and the gap between us and the green truck widened, but not for long. The Ford swung out as though to pass. When its nose drew even with our rear wheel the driver cranked it into our lane, but Jean-Marie floored the Dodge van and we shot forward just in time. The velocity pressed against my chest like a hand. The green truck moved back into the left lane, and I watched over my shoulder as it slowly gained on us. We flew along, seemingly in formation, at almost impossible speeds down the long empty road. A reflection of the clouds scrolled up the truck's windshield, and it seemed like we were being pursued by a manic sky.

Our little suburban van was reaching its limits and had started to vibrate. Jean-Marie urged it on under his breath, but it was no match for the powerful truck. The passenger window on the Ford rolled down, and a long dark tube emerged. I cried out. Jean-Marie glanced quickly in his side mirror.

"*Merde!*" Jean-Marie slowed slightly. My mouth opened in protest. "Hold on," he said.

The green truck was now alongside, and the long dark tube slowly swung towards us. Jean-Marie braked hard, and I pitched forward. The Ford shot past. I heard a sharp crack, and a small geyser of dirt spurted up a few feet in front of us. Jean-Marie steered sharply to the left, then back to the right, and the Dodge van fishtailed in a dizzying turn. I lurched from one side to the other. My seat belt jerked tight, but not before my head grazed the window on my door, gently, like an echo.

Jean-Marie stomped on the gas, and we headed back in the direction of Chibougamau. We had driven for only a couple of minutes when he slowed the van to a crawl and made a lazy U-turn. A Jeep that had come up behind us tooted its horn at this minor infraction as it passed by. Jean-Marie accelerated, and we headed back in the direction from which we had just come.

"What are you doing?" I said.

"Trust me," Jean-Marie said, his eyes intent on the road.

A small dark spot appeared at the point where the road met the horizon. It slowly grew in size.

"They have a gun," I said. "They shot at us."

"Yes, I know."

The Ford was now clearly identifiable and advancing towards us, not as quickly as during the chase but with steady purpose. When it was about five hundred feet away, Jean-Marie swung our van into the left lane.

I sat silent, frozen with shock. The seconds passed, each as taut as a stretched rubber band. One, two, three, four. The distance between our van and the Ford rapidly closed. The detailing on the Ford's grille was now clear. I concentrated on trying to read the numbers and letters on the truck's licence plate as they became legible. I recognized an *M* and an *X* and what was either a *B* or an *8*.

Tires squealed, and the green truck twisted into the ditch. It hit the far bank and spiralled into the air, rolling three times before it settled on its roof and rocked for a moment, a mass of twisted metal. Steam or smoke issued from somewhere beneath it.

Jean-Marie had slowed down for the few seconds it had all taken to happen to watch the truck's fate in his side mirror. He turned back to the front, his face grim, pulled into the right lane, and pressed on the gas.

As the miles passed, the shock slowly subsided and I was suddenly seized by a violent nausea. "Stop, please, you have to stop," I said. I covered my mouth and bowed my head.

Jean-Marie slowed and pulled to the shoulder. I fumbled with the clip of the seat belt and scrabbled at the handle of my door. When it opened, I spilled out and fell to my hands and knees. My gut convulsed, and I spewed out half-digested oatmeal and yoghurt. Even when there was nothing left, my stomach still heaved. When I finally stopped, I sat up in a crouch, panting. I felt a hand on my shoulder.

"Here," Jean-Marie said.

I took the bottle of water, drank, and spat. I rinsed my mouth again, then swallowed. Jean-Marie gave me his hand and pulled me to my feet.

"Are you okay?"

I drew in a deep breath and nodded. "I'll survive."

"We should go."

We sped along without speaking for a long time. I finally broke the silence. "All this wilderness, we would have just disappeared."

"Yes, probably."

"Where did you learn how to drive like that?"

"In Africa," Jean-Marie said. "I learned many things in Africa."

"What if they had called your bluff?"

Jean-Marie's forehead wrinkled. "What is to 'call a bluff'?"

"What if they hadn't gone off the road?"

"It is the natural thing to do. It is instinct. The driver, he would not think, he would just act."

I persisted. "But what if he hadn't swerved?"

"Then I would go back into my lane."

"And if he had gone into your lane?"

"Well, naturally, I would go straight."

"You could have reacted that quickly?"

"Yes."

I didn't speak for a moment. "That was a dangerous game you played."

Jean-Marie glanced at me. "Yes," he said quietly, "but it was my game."

Chapter 13

Jean-Marie and I caught a connector from Chicoutimi to Montreal with minutes to spare, and I was able to change our reservations to depart for Vancouver later that day. While we waited for the flight, I paced the airport concourse trying to calm jangled nerves. Jean-Marie went to a bar in the departure zone and drank steadily.

Because of our last-minute booking, we weren't able to sit together. Jean-Marie took an inside seat three rows ahead of mine, tucked a pillow between his head and the window, and slept through the flight. At Vancouver, we transferred to the shuttle to the Victoria airport and landed in time to make the last ferry to South Salish.

After a clipped goodbye, Jean-Marie strode off the ferry ahead of me. In one of our few exchanges during the return trip, he said that Jasmine would be there to drive him home. Weary after the long hours of travel, I followed more slowly to where Kate was waiting for me in the parking lot.

***

"Complicated. I'm still processing it all," I said to Kate when she asked me how the trip had gone.

Kate was expecting a full house for the weekend, so when we arrived at her place she set me up in Everett's room. Hugh wasn't around, and when I asked after him Kate said that he was suffering one of the periodic relapses characteristic of his condition. Looking at her more closely, I saw that her eyes were bruised with fatigue.

"Kate, maybe I should go back to the cabin. I don't want to be yet another burden or intrude on you and Hugh."

"No, hon, we love having you. It can get pretty desolate, just the two of us. It's why we've done the B&B. With people around, we have less time to dwell on, well, on our situation."

"Are you sure? I'd hate to wear out my welcome," I said. *Or lose you as friends,* I thought. I was suddenly struck by how close I felt to these people, how much they had come to matter to me in such a short time.

Kate offered something approaching her usual smile. "If there's any danger of that, I'll let you know."

Over the next couple of days, I had little time alone with Kate. With the guests coming and going and having to be fed, there was constantly something to do, and she spent any free time taking care of Hugh. She had readily accepted my offer of help, but when she suggested I make the morning muffins I put my hands up in alarm and said I would clean the guest rooms.

I was grateful for the distraction that stripping beds, scrubbing sinks, and doing laundry provided from the horror of the Chibougamau experience. Still, it played on an endless loop at the back of my mind. Had the bad business in Vancouver followed me there, or were its roots in fact in Chibougamau? I suspected the latter. Was it just my presence that had prompted the car chase, or had some of my questions unwittingly strayed into dangerous territory? What frustrated me most was that despite the risks we had taken and our harrowing escape, my inquiries had been fruitless: I was no closer to knowing what I was involved in or who was after me.

Then there was Leo. I had found out significant, life-defining things about his past, but it seemed that the more I learned, the less I knew him. Why had he never told me about his family, Mario, his mother, about Sardinia? What did that say about our relationship? I had anticipated spending my life with this man; had I been totally deluded about the sincerity of his feelings for me?

And Nick Duvall? Leo's ties to him were equally puzzling. The episode at the gas station had been a critical juncture in the Barsoni family's life, and Nick had been at the heart of it. Although it was a strong connection between them, it explained neither why Nick had come after Leo twenty-five years later nor why he had demanded money.

Finally, I couldn't help but wonder what had happened to the occupants of the truck we had forced off the road. As Jean-Marie and I had approached a small town on the road back to Chicoutimi, I had suggested that we stop and report the accident. Jean-Marie had given me an incredulous look and said no. The act had been, without question, one of self-defense, a matter of us or them, but it gnawed at my conscience.

***

I didn't get a chance to debrief Kate and Hugh on the trip until late Sunday afternoon after Kate had seen off the last of the guests, a young couple wearing anoraks and hiking boots and carrying heavy backpacks. As she poured out cups of coffee, Hugh wheeled himself into the kitchen looking wan but determinedly upright. They listened to my account, gasping with shock when I mentioned the car chase—an abbreviated version omitting Jean-Marie's manoeuvre—and murmuring with sympathy as I spoke of my bewilderment and hurt over Leo's secrecy.

"Clare ..."—Hugh hesitated before continuing—"is it possible that you are looking at this wrong?"

"What do you mean?"

"Mario died because of Duvall's violent temper. Could it have been Leo who was after Duvall, not the other way around?"

I thought for a moment. "You mean that maybe Leo had been nursing his vengeance all the years Duvall was in prison, and when he was finally free, Leo lured him out to Vancouver, say, by offering him money, with the intent of executing his own form of justice? Or satisfying some obscure code of honour?"

"But then somehow the tables turned and Duvall nailed Leo instead," Hugh said.

"And Duvall, being the ruthless and conniving person he was, tried to turn the situation to his advantage by making out that Leo owed him money," I said.

"Disturbing as it sounds, it also fits with the facts."

I folded my arms on the table and gazed without focus at its wood grain while I considered what Hugh was suggesting. After a couple of minutes, I leaned back and said, "You know, not long ago I would have said that this was totally out of character for Leo, but now I don't know what to think. Even if it was true, though, it still doesn't explain who then killed Duvall and why, now, they're after me."

"That's another thing you could look at differently," Hugh said. "Maybe Duvall's murder has nothing to do with his business with Leo. Duvall was killed not long after he had been in Chibougamau. It could have been related to something he had done there, and whoever killed him thought you were his associate, a notion you reinforced by going back to Chibougamau and asking a bunch of questions. Maybe that's why you're a target."

"One way or another, I'm no further ahead than I was before Chibougamau." I rubbed my face, overwhelmed by the whole thing. "I have no idea what to do next."

"Well, there's Leo's mother. Could she still be alive?" Kate said.

"I've been wondering about that," I said. "And about what prompted their decision to split up. Leo was still in his teens. Why wouldn't he have gone back to Sardinia with his mom?"

Kate leaned forward. "Maybe you need to find her, hon. Could be she knows what this is all about."

"I thought Leo's mother died when he was a child. At least, that's what he told me," Karen said when I called to inquire about what she knew of Leo's family.

"He told me the same thing, but it appears not to be the case."

"Well, she's probably dead now." Karen sounded inexplicably cross about the matter, as if she had just found out that Leo had cheated on her or something.

"She'd be only in her sixties or seventies, so there's a good chance she's still alive. If that's the case, I'd like to meet her. Can you help at all?"

"It's not going to be easy."

"I know."

"And it's going to cost."

"I understand."

Karen's sigh fluttered through the receiver, and I heard the complaint of a drawer being opened. "I know a lawyer in Italy, someone I met at a conference in Geneva, who may be able to help."

***

Jean-Marie didn't come to work the Monday after we returned. I thought nothing of it until he didn't show up again on the Tuesday. Jasmine did instead. I sat down with her in Kate's lounge. The day was warm, and the empty fireplace struck a dismal note in the sunlit space.

Jasmine was like a black and white photo of herself, her usual vibrancy muted. She wore a shapeless beige sweater over faded jeans and scuffed boots and sat gazing out the window, her hands picking at each other in her lap.

"You wanted to see me?" I prompted after we had sat in silence for a few minutes.

Jasmine turned to me. "I want to know what went on in Chibougamau."

I started. Had Jasmine found out about my staying in Jean-Marie's room? Had she heard my hysterical laughter when they were speaking on the telephone? "I, uh, don't know what you mean."

"Something happened there. I want to know what it was."

"What has Jean-Marie told you?" I said cautiously.

Jasmine's eyes filled with tears. "That's just it. He hasn't told me anything. He has barely spoken at all since he returned." She swallowed. "Every so often, he goes through a bad time. He has ... ghosts, something from his past that seizes him. He has never told me what it is, but when it happens it can be days when he just lies around, doesn't talk, barely eats. I've seen it before, but it frightens Mischa. It used to happen more often but not so much since we've been here. I thought it was all over, finally past, but ..." She shook her head, drew a voluminous sleeve across her eyes. "Something happened out there. If I knew what it was, maybe I could talk him through it."

I recalled the silent, feral-eyed stranger sporting a two-day beard and smelling of stale red wine who had returned home with me, so different from the self-contained, assured man with whom I had left.

"Something did happen in Chibougamau," I said slowly. I told her about the car chase, this time including Jean-Marie's manoeuvre that forced our pursuers off the road. "He probably saved my life."

"Yes, but it may have been at the expense of his own," Jasmine said, eyes flashing.

"I had no idea. I'm so sorry."

Jasmine drew in a long breath and stood up. "At least I can try to talk to him now."

I rose and followed her to the front door. "Can I help at all? Please let me know if I can do anything, if you need anything."

Jasmine arched one brow. "I think you've done enough already." She opened the door and was gone.

***

Jean-Marie showed up two days later. After checking in with Dak, with whom he had left a list of jobs to be done, he came over to Kate and Hugh's. I had been waiting for him ever since Hugh mentioned seeing his truck earlier in the morning, and opened the door before he could knock.

"Come in, please," I said. I anxiously searched his face for an indication of his state of mind.

"No, it is okay. I just want to say that I am back."

"Jean-Marie … I'm very sorry for what happened in Chibougamau. I never expected it would come to that. If I had known, I would never have exposed you to such danger. But I don't know what I would have done if you hadn't been there."

"It is okay." Jean-Marie said, his old self lurking somewhere in the depths of his eyes. He smiled wryly. "It made for a change from the vineyard."

"What are you going to do now?"

Jean-Marie gestured at the farm. "Work, of course. There is much to do, and we are behind."

***

Not knowing how long it would take for Karen's contact in Italy to get the information, if he was able to at all, I decided that it was time to move back to my cabin. When I mentioned this to Kate and Hugh, they exchanged a glance and Hugh cleared his throat and said, "I haven't wanted to alarm you, but I get a good view of road traffic from my office, and there is a big SUV, a dark grey one, that drives back and forth several times a day. I could be imagining things, but it seems to slow down when it goes past your place."

"Oh," I said. I was quiet for a moment. "It might be best if I found somewhere else to stay. I may be putting you two in danger as well."

"Don't worry, hon," Kate said, "I've got my gun."

My eyes just about popped out of my head. "Your *what?*"

Hugh made a calming gesture. "It's just a twenty-two rifle. Annie Oakley here figured she needed it living in the country."

"But, Kate ... Where did you learn how to shoot?"

Kate shrugged. "Hon, everybody in Texas knows how to shoot."

***

Seven days later, Karen called me to report that her lawyer friend in Italy had proved to be surprisingly productive and, working through a private investigator on Sardinia, had been able to find the information I was seeking.

"I was frankly astonished at how quickly I got a response," she said. "I didn't expect anything for weeks, if ever. But I guess that Sardinia is not a very big place."

"What did they find out?"

"It seems that Leo's mother is in fact still alive. The private investigator was able to track her down through the vital statistics and other registers. It's easier now that they are computerized. She has remarried and lives in a town called San Teodoro."

When I didn't speak for several moments, Karen said, "Are you still there?"

"Yes, sorry. I'm just thinking."

"What do you want to do now? Do you want those fellows to make any further inquiries?"

"I think ..." I paused for several moments, then took a deep breath. "I want to meet her, Karen. Can you get them to arrange it?"

***

My meeting with Leo's mother came about in an unexpected way. Four days after speaking to Karen, I received a telephone call from a young woman named Andrea Vitale. Speaking in precise English with a vaguely British accent, she introduced herself as the niece of

Signora Gisela Vitale and said that she understood I had asked to meet with her aunt. Before she would agree to the meeting, her aunt wished to better understand who I was and what I wanted to speak to her about.

I told Andrea about my connection to Leo and his death, and explained that I hoped to meet any remaining family he may have. Andrea expressed neither surprise nor curiosity at my introduction.

"I see. I will speak to my aunt and call you again," she said, and hung up.

Andrea called again two days later. "My aunt does not see the value of your travelling all this way to see her, but she will meet with you if you do. You are welcome to come and take coffee with her when you arrive. When will you be here?"

"As soon as I am able to make arrangements. Can I call to let you know?" I scribbled down the telephone number Andrea gave me as well as the street address of Leo's mother's place in San Teodoro.

***

The trip to Sardinia required that I retrieve my passport from the condo. I directed the taxi that had brought me from the floatplane to the rear entrance, slipped into the elevator, and exited on my floor, releasing a great sigh of relief that no one appeared to have witnessed my arrival.

I approached my door with my eyes focused on the small piece of paper where I had written the code to my lock, so I didn't see that the device had been pried away from the door until I reached out to touch the keypad. You wouldn't have noticed from a distance because the gap was just wide enough to allow a narrow instrument to slide in. I pulled my hand slowly back as though the disabled lock were radioactive. When my thoughts caught up with my trembling body, my first instinct was to run, and I did in fact back up several paces. I stopped and stared at the door. *What now?* I thought. *What do they want now?*

I heard the elevator cables rattling as it approached my floor and held my breath, hoping it wouldn't stop. It did, and I gathered myself up to flee or fight as I waited for the doors to open. I relaxed when one of my neighbours emerged, an older man who lived across the hall. I stepped back towards my door and pretended to be fiddling with the keypad. We exchanged greetings as he passed.

"Haven't seen you for a while," the man said. He wiggled his key into his deadbolt. "By the way," he said over his shoulder, "how do you like that electronic lock?"

"Fine," I said, "just fine." I twisted the doorknob and entered the condo.

I stood in the dim hall, breathing in the smell of dust and warm, stale air, listening for any indication that someone else was present. The silence had the flat quality of absence. After a few moments, I stepped further into the hall and turned on the light. There had been a painting on the wall at the end of the hallway, an abstract with bold splashes of primary colours, red, yellow, blue. It was still there, but pieces of the canvas now hung like pendants. Someone had slashed a large X across its face.

I turned into the living room. All the other paintings there had received the same treatment and hung in shreds. The sofa as well; great Xs carved into the seat and back cushions. And the armchairs. I moved like an automaton through the rest of the unit. All other paintings and soft chairs had been sliced with the vicious X. Jean-Marie would have said that the nature of the destruction bore a message. I was pretty sure I knew what it was.

I came out of my trance long enough to fish my passport out of the filing cabinet where it was stored. Then I left, closing the door behind me, not caring that the place was unlocked. What else could anyone do now?

I exited the condo by the front door, blind, now, to any threat. A taxi was dropping someone off at the entrance. I hurried to it, climbed in, and asked the driver to take me to the airport. The shock hit me as we pulled away from the curb, and I began to cry, a hard, silent outpouring. The taxi driver, a black man with Rasta hair caught up in a blue and orange knitted cap, caught my eye in the rear-view mirror.

"Lady, you leave your man?"

I bent my head, covered my face with my hands.

"Hey, good to cry. But, you know, it be better soon."

***

I sat, dry-eyed and unsleeping, through the overnight flight to Italy, wondering how things could ever be better. An image persisted in my mind: a line of fish of decreasing size, each with its mouth open to eat the smaller one before it. And I was the littlest fish. Nick Duvall had tried to swallow me, but some bigger fish got to him first, and now I was next in line.

The destruction in the condo could have happened at any time in the weeks since I had been there last, but I had no doubt it was done after the events at Chibougamau. Tit for tat. Whoever was behind it was seriously annoyed and had a very long reach. I had eluded them so far by staying out of sight at Kate and Hugh's, but they were obviously resourceful, and it was just a matter of time before they found me there. I knuckled my aching eyes. How on earth was I going to fix this?

Chapter 14

I had wisely arranged to spend a day and night in Milan before carrying on to Sardinia. The next morning, after a long, exhausted sleep, I caught the short flight to the small city of Olbia on the northeast coast of Sardinia. San Teodoro was a half hour drive away.

I had hired a car and driver for the day at the Olbia airport. The driver, I was assured, spoke some English. He did sufficiently well to understand my instructions but not to converse, so we rode in silence. I hadn't travelled much, and by any standard the landscape we drove through was beautiful. The fields were lush with purple, white, and yellow flowers, and in the distance the Mediterranean shaded from turquoise near the shore to a heartbreaking ultramarine towards the horizon.

The address in San Teodoro that Andrea had given me was on a side street that curved off the main road to follow the contour of the sloping land. It belonged to a two-storey inn with ochre stucco walls and a red tiled roof. A covered terrace on one side faced a garden enclosed by a wall with the same stucco finish as the building. On the second floor, small wrought iron balconies projected out from tall narrow French doors at about twenty-foot intervals. Black planters spilling over with multi-coloured flowers suspended from the balcony railings added a festive note.

When I presented myself at the front desk of the inn, a short dark-haired woman in a red and white patterned dress rose from a leather armchair in the small lobby.

"I am Andrea," she said, extending her hand. She was in her mid-twenties, and a long, sharp nose detracted from what would otherwise have been a pretty face. "Please come this way," she said, turning.

I followed the black velvet bow that bobbed at her neck through an arch at the end of the lobby to the glass-enclosed terrace. Several people were seated at tables with colourful mosaic tops having lunch, and their chatter filled the room, its cadence foreign. Doors on the wall facing the garden were folded back, and floral and cut-grass scents mingled with the tantalizing aromas of roasted tomatoes and blistered-crust pizza.

Andrea led me through the doors to a white wrought iron table tucked in a corner of the garden under a trellis over which rampaged a blossom-heavy bougainvillea vine. The woman who sat at the table was, by my calculation, in her late sixties or early seventies, but slate-grey hair and a softened jawline were her only concessions to advancing age. Diamond studs flashed in her ears as she turned to watch our approach.

Andrea introduced us, and I extended my hand across the small round table. Signora Vitale touched my fingers briefly with the tips of her own. She said something to Andrea in Italian. Andrea nodded and left us. I watched Andrea go with some apprehension. How would Signora Vitale and I converse?

"Please, sit," Signora Vitale said, indicating the only other chair.

As I did, a young, slender man in black trousers and a white shirt appeared with a loaded tray and, with liquid movements, set coffee service, glasses of water, and a plate of pale, oblong biscuits on the table. While he poured out the coffee into eggshell-thin cups,

Signora Vitale studied me with interest. I remembered Monsieur Godbout referring to her as "Sophia Loren." There was no particular similarity that I could see between the two women beyond dark eyes under fine, arched brows and a certain self-possession.

"You have come a long way," Signora Vitale said after the server had tucked his silver tray under his arm and left. Her deep, amber-toned voice amplified her accent.

"Yes, and I am very happy that you speak English. With all the travel arrangements, I had forgotten that I might need a translator."

Signora Vitale may have smiled, but it came and went so quickly I couldn't be sure. "I was a schoolteacher when I was young. It is what I taught. So what is it that you want from me?"

"I thought that with Leo dead, it would be nice to meet his family. Also, he left me with some, um, unfinished business, matters that I need some information about his background, his time growing up in Chibougamau, to resolve."

Signora Vitale dropped a sugar cube in her cup and stirred it with a miniature spoon. "How did he die?"

"He was killed in a car accident."

Signora Vitale nodded, her expression flat, her eyes unreadable.

"If you don't mind my saying so, you don't seem to be particularly distressed by your son's death," I said, but gently.

Signora Vitale eyed me curiously. "Leonardo was not my son."

I had drunk some coffee and the cup clattered when I put it back in the saucer.

"Did Leonardo say I was his mother?"

My jet-lagged brain struggled to make sense of her words, and I didn't answer immediately. "No," I finally said, "Leo never referred to you at all. I learned about you only when I visited Chibougamau and spoke to people who had known you there."

"Ah." The fleeting smile came and went again. "What do you want to know?"

"Well …," I said, a bit dazed. "Maybe we can start with Leo's mother: Who was she, what happened to her, and how do you fit in?"

Signora Vitale took a delicate sip of coffee and explained. Leo was the son of her first husband, Paolo Barsoni, and his first wife. His mother died when he was four years old. Signora Vitale married Signor Barsoni two years later.

I frowned. "Then, Mario …"

Signora Vitale lifted her chin. "Yes, I had a child also, Mario. He needed a father."

I spent a brief moment contemplating what life as an unmarried mother would have been like here all those years ago. "What brought you to Canada?"

"Life was very hard then; there was not much work here. After Mario, I could not work as a teacher anymore. Many people were going to America, and Paolo said that maybe we should go." She shrugged. "'Why not?' I thought. I knew how to speak English; it would be easy. And Mario's father was American, from Chicago. I thought maybe I could find him, show him that he had a son.

"But Paolo had worked in the mines here in Sardinia, and there were mining jobs in Canada. So we went to this place, and it was like the end of the world. It was so cold." She shuddered and gathered the pale blue cardigan she wore more tightly over her white silk blouse.

"And they did not even speak English there, just French. Just French. Ten years I was there. They were very long years."

Yes, I thought, looking around the lush garden, noisy with life and colour, *living in northern Canada would have taken some adjustment after the Mediterranean.* "I can see that it would have been difficult," I said.

We sat in silence for several moments, Signora Vitale lost in her memories, turning the tiny spoon round and round in her fingers.

"What can you tell me about Leo?" I said.

Signora Vitale glanced up at me from under her brows. "Ah, Leonardo …" She blew out a dismissive puff of air. "He was a dull boy. So ordinary, you would not notice him. Not like my Mario. Mario, so beautiful with his wavy hair, his long eyelashes. How the

girls loved him. And always one for fun. He laughed all the time."
She winced, her eyes full of pain.

My blood rose at Signora Vitale's casual dismissal of Leo. "But then Mario died, didn't he?"

Signora Vitale's head jerked back, and she considered me for a moment with narrowed eyes.

"I'm sorry to be so direct, but that's what I want to find out about, how it happened, what you and Leo did after."

"Leonardo did not tell you?"

I shook my head.

"Maybe he forgot; maybe it didn't matter anymore." Signora Vitale laughed bitterly. "But then he never had anything to say, even when it was important."

"Will you tell me?" I prompted.

She looked at me sharply. "You ask for much."

"I know. I ask it of you as a kindness."

Signora Vitale sighed and looked at a point somewhere over my left shoulder. "There is never a day when I do not think about what happened. But I have spoken of it only once, to my husband." She turned back to me. "Tell me, again, why you want to know."

"Nick Duvall caused Leo's death."

Signora Vitale's eyes widened. She exhaled sharply and shook her head. "I never thought to hear that name again. And he is making trouble for you?" I nodded, but before I could tell her Nick was dead, she said, "Then yes, okay, I will tell you."

She spoke of that fateful night, the same events, the same players Luc Brossard had mentioned, but, like with a twist of a kaleidoscope, arranged into a different pattern. It was just before Christmas. Mario had gone out with Nick Duvall and Robert Fournier that night. Robert was in trouble at university and needed money.

"For drugs maybe, or poker; they liked to play poker," she said.

Nick had the idea to rob the old man who owned the hardware store in town when the man went, as he always did, to put the day's earnings in the bank's night deposit box. The store had been busy with Christmas shopping, and Nick figured there would be a lot of money. I recalled Luc Brossard mentioning the incident, one of the many that had happened on the night when Mario was fatally injured. My mind searched for the old man's name: Didier.

Mario had been reluctant, but the other two bullied him into coming along. Signora Vitale shook her head. "All you do is keep watch, they said."

They had planned to grab the money and run. They wrapped their scarves high around their faces so no one would know who they were, but old man Didier had unexpectedly fought back and, in the ensuing tussle, pulled off Robert Fournier's scarf.

"Of course, the mayor's son, no one could know it was him," Signora Vitale said, her lip curling.

Robert had panicked and pushed Didier over, then Nick Duvall got into the act. They kicked the old man until he was still, and then Nick stomped on his face.

"Mario tried to stop them, but ..." She shrugged and sighed. When it was over, Robert and Nick pulled the old man into a dark corner and they all ran away.

"Mario wanted to go home, but Robert said that they needed a story for when the police found the old man."

It had been Robert's idea to go to the gas station. They knew that the boy from the gas station—the name Desjardin came into my mind unbidden—would be working that night, and they planned to make a disturbance, nothing serious, but enough to bring the police. When the police found them there, they wouldn't connect them to the old man.

But then, as I knew, things got out of hand at the gas station. When the police came, they took all three, Nick, Robert, and Mario, to the station and threw them into a cell. There had been some other trouble (the crazy Potvins, I remembered), and the police decided to release Robert and Mario as soon as a police car was available to take them home. Nick had to stay in jail because he was the one who had been fighting and Mr. Desjardin was pressing charges.

When Mario was dropped off at their house, Leo was there alone. There had been a Christmas party at the office where Signora Vitale cleaned, and she returned home later than usual and went straight to bed. The next morning, she cooked some breakfast and went to the room Leo and Mario shared to tell them to come and eat.

"I could not wake Mario. He was limp and heavy, like a sack of sand." She drew her fingers down her cheeks. "And his face, it was the colour of cold ashes." Her eyes filled.

Leo had woken up, and when he saw Mario he said that they should get him to the hospital. He rushed to the house next door in his pajamas and returned with the neighbour. They managed to bundle Mario into the neighbour's car. Signora Vitale accompanied Mario, leaving Leo to dress and follow on foot.

At the hospital, the emergency room doctor wasn't able to determine what the problem was. It was only when Leo arrived that they learned how Mario had been injured. The doctor quickly concluded that Mario's spleen had been ruptured and required surgery.

"But it was too late; they could not save him." Signora Vitale's mouth crumpled, and she beat her fist against her heart.

I reached out to touch Signora Vitale's hand but stopped; she would not welcome the intimacy. We sat without speaking until Signora Vitale had composed herself.

"If you could not wake Mario up, how did you know what had happened?" I said.

"Leonardo knew what happened. Mario told him. He said he did not tell me right away because it was a secret and he did not want to get Mario into trouble." Signora Vitale leaned forward and spoke fiercely. "But Leonardo should have known better. If he had told me that Mario was sick when I came home from work that night, if he had told me what had happened when I tried to wake Mario in the morning, Mario could have been saved. But ..."—Signora Vitale's voice cracked—"that stupid, stupid boy, he did not tell me."

We sat staring at each other in silence for a long moment, Signora Vitale's chest rising and falling with emotion. I sighed. "What happened next?"

"I buried my son, then I left that terrible place and came home, here to Sardinia. I wanted to go when Paolo died, I should have, but Mario said, no, no, that place was his home now."

"Did Leo not want to go with you?"

Signora Vitale made a contemptuous motion with her hand. "I was angry, so angry. I told him I never wanted to see him again."

"But he was only seventeen."

Signora Vitale glared at me, her eyes as hard and bright as the diamonds in her ears. She jerked her face away and said, "*Basta!* That is enough. You should go now."

I nodded and gathered up my bag. "Please, one thing more. Why didn't you tell the police about the old man?"

Signora Vitale dismissed the question with a wave of her hand. "What, and have them think Mario did something bad?"

"Then what happened to the money Mario's friends had stolen?"

Signora Vitale jaw set at my presumption, but she answered. "Mario didn't want any of the money, but at the police station Nick said to keep his share for him so the police would not find it. I guess he did not trust Robert. I told Leonardo to burn the money. My son was not a thief."

The last pieces of the puzzle clicked into place. I stood up. "Thank you," I said softly, and left.

***

Signora Vitale's revelations tumbled through my mind on the long flight home. I had gone to Sardinia in pursuit of an enigma and found a tragedy. Leo honours Mario's confidence, but the act of loyalty leads to his stepbrother's death. Mario's mother, blinded by grief, blames Leo for her son's death and casts him out. I tried to muster indignation over Signora Vitale's treatment of Leo but could only work up a feeling of profound sadness. Had she ever regretted leaving Leo behind? It seemed not. Apart from asking how he died, she had expressed no interest in what had happened to him, about his life, and her anger and resentment at his role in Mario's death were still fresh and raw.

Then there was Leo. What a burden he must have carried with Mario's death and his own role in it. The shared secret and Leo's attempt to keep his stepbrother out of trouble suggested that the boys were close. The loss of Mario, so soon after Leo's father died, must have been devastating. Add to this rejection by the only mother he would have known. Given Leo's silence on the matter of his family, he must have been deeply scarred by these events. It explained much about him: his solitary life, his secrets, even the time it had taken him to commit to our relationship. It hurt to know that he not trusted me enough to reveal this painful part of his past. Or had he buried it so deep that it was no longer part of who he was? Nick Duvall's sudden appearance would have ripped those wounds wide open again. *We have to talk,* Leo had said on that last night. Had he intended to open up to me?

And I finally had an explanation for why Nick Duvall had come after Leo—to reclaim his share from that fateful robbery. It would have been Nick's first chance to do so. After being taken into custody on that night, he did not leave prison again until he was released last fall.

My guess was that Leo hadn't burned the money as his stepmother had instructed. It may have been simple necessity; from what Gilles and the Godbouts had said, the Barsoni family had had little money and Signora Vitale may have left Leo with nothing when she went away. Or perhaps Leo had assumed Mario's commitment to hold Nick's share of the money until he was out of jail. Or, it may have been as simple as not wanting to cross Nick Duvall.

Whatever Leo's reason for hanging on to Nick's take from the robbery, he had kept it separate and secret, probably because he didn't consider it his. Which meant the money wasn't really mine, either. I put that matter aside to deal with later because I had something more pressing to consider: I finally understood who was after me and why.

Chapter 15

When I arrived back in Vancouver, I checked into a hotel at the airport and passed the night in fitful sleep. The next morning I telephoned Inspector Yuen.

"What's up?" Yuen said when he came on the line.

"I have some new information for you concerning the death of Nick Duvall."

"Duvall?" Yuen was silent for a few moments, poking around through his memory, perhaps. "Right. I'm tied up right now, but come by this afternoon."

At the police station, I had to wait for Inspector Yuen to complete a phone call. When I was eventually admitted, Yuen's harried appearance and distraction made it clear that my visit was an unwelcome interruption. Even his silky voice sounded like someone had rubbed it over with sandpaper, but the balls of used tissues on his desk explained why. He swept the tissues into a garbage can beside his desk, motioned me into the visitors' chair, dropped down into his own, and said, "Okay, so what's this new information?"

I perched on the rickety chair and tucked my suitcase in the gap between it and the wall. "I went to Chibougamau a couple of weeks ago," I said.

"Chibougamau?" Yuen's forehead puckered. "That's where Duvall came from, right?"

I nodded.

"And you were doing what, exactly, there?"

Here goes, I thought. "It's where Leo grew up. We had always planned to go there." My cheeks reddened at the blatant lie. "And I thought, now that he's gone, it would be kind of interesting to see the town."

"And while Leo lived in this town, did he happen to know Nick Duvall?"

"Well, sort of."

"And when did you become aware of this?" Yuen's voice was very, very even.

I swallowed. "Actually, it was when you mentioned that Nick Duvall came from Chibougamau, when we were talking at the RCMP office on South Salish, after that Russian guy was found dead at my place."

"And it didn't occur to you that I would be interested in knowing that Nick Duvall and your boyfriend were from the same town?"

I had no answer to this, so I stayed silent.

Inspector Yuen leaned forward on his desk and fixed me with a hard stare. His face crumpled, and he snatched a tissue from a box on his desk to cover a sneeze. When he disposed of the tissue, he sniffed and said, "You know, I've had just about enough of you. I've given you a lot of leeway. A lot of cops, they would have had you up for both the Duvall murder and the Melnikov death, but I thought, 'She's a nice lady. She's gotten mixed up in some of her boyfriend's business, but she's not responsible, probably doesn't even know what's going on,' and here you do this to me!"

I shrank into my chair. "I'm sorry. I guess I was afraid that you'd find out something about Leo, and with him dead, I didn't think that it mattered what, if anything, he may have done."

"We have a murder to solve!"

"Well, Leo could hardly have done it, and I know I didn't."

Yuen leaned back in his chair and shook his head. "So what is it you want to tell me?"

I delivered a crisp report on what I had learned in Chibougamau and from Leo's mother in Sardinia. "So I think that it's this politician who is behind Nick Duvall's murder. Duvall may have been blackmailing him, threatening to expose him. And he's probably also the one who sent Melnikov after me. He probably figures that because I was with Nick Duvall I know something. Well, I guess I do, now."

When I was done, Yuen stared incredulously at me. "So you think some high-ranking politico from the other side of the country is mucking around over here, getting people killed in the street and having you followed?"

"Yes, I do."

Yuen's eyebrows were threatening his hairline. "I've never heard such a load of ... nonsense."

I straightened up in my chair. "But I talked to people who knew what happened!"

"How long ago was this? Twenty-five years? Do you know how many people can't accurately remember what happened yesterday, let alone twenty-five years ago?"

"For some of them, it's the kind of thing you can't ever forget."

Yuen grabbed a tissue from the box on his desk and muffled another sneeze. He blew his nose and pitched the tissue in the direction of his wastebasket without looking. "Were any of these people who you talked to actually there when this supposed murder of the old man happened?"

"Well, no. The people who were there, except for Robert Fournier, are all dead."

"So it's only the mother of this Mario guy, Leo's stepbrother or whatever, who claims to know what supposedly happened?"

I nodded.

"And you believe her account?"

"I don't see any reason not to."

"And she basically says everyone else did something bad but her son. How do you know it wasn't actually her son who killed the old guy?"

I thought of the fierce, proud woman who thought the sun had risen and set with her son. Yes, she could certainly have framed her recollection to Mario's credit. *My son is not a thief,* she had said. Was he a murderer?

Inspector Yuen was still talking. "I'm not saying Duvall was an angel. I wouldn't be surprised if he was involved in some way."

"Yes, and that's why he was after Leo. He wanted his share of the money they had stolen."

Inspector Yuen cocked an eyebrow. "From what we saw, your friend Leo wouldn't have had too much trouble paying Duvall off. I still think there was something else going on."

I slumped back in my chair. "But then how do you explain why someone would kill Duvall and why Valerian Melnikov was after me?"

Inspector Yuen studied me for a moment. "Look, what I've concluded is that there was some business between Duvall and the Russian mafia, probably something from Duvall's time in prison, that led Melnikov to kill him, and that you were in the wrong place at the wrong time, and Melnikov figured you knew something, and that's why he was after you. Then Melnikov got himself killed at your place, and I actually don't care how that happened—"

"I wasn't responsible!"

Yuen raised his palm. "Whatever, good riddance to bad rubbish, I say. Anyhow, with Melnikov gone now, I figure it's all over and I'm ready to close the file on Duvall."

"But it's not all over! Someone is still after me."

Yuen looked at me cross-eyed as he blew his nose. "Oh, come on."

"No, really. In Chibougamau, someone broke into my hotel room and trashed the place, and they took a notebook I had."

"Did you report it to the police there?"

"No."

Yuen shook his head and made an exasperated noise.

"And then someone …" I stopped. I could hardly tell Yuen about the guys in the big green truck who had chased Jean-Marie and me out of Chibougamau, given how we had driven them off the road. I leaned forward. "Anyhow, when I came back to my condo last week, the lock was broken and all the paintings inside were slashed."

"Did you call it in?"

"No, I was too upset and I didn't have time. You can go and look if you don't believe me."

Yuen threw up his hands. "So what makes you think that these things have anything to do with Duvall or Melnikov?"

"Why else would they have happened?"

Yuen shook his head. "Look, Clare, I think you've got an overactive imagination. Playing at detective, stringing a whole bunch of stuff together, adding up two and two and getting five. Understandable, sure, with what you've been through, but really. Maybe you need to talk to someone, get some counselling."

I stared at Yuen, speechless. He looked at his watch without bothering to conceal the action. "So you're not going to do anything with what I've told you," I said. Shock had knotted my voice into a squeak.

Yuen sighed. "Look, I'm sorry, but I just don't buy this business with the political guy. As far as the death of that old man in Chibougamau, all you've given me is a bunch of hearsay that I can't do anything with. If something happened, it was years ago and thousands of miles outside of my jurisdiction. I won't even mention the fact that it would mean taking on a high-flying politician. A thankless task at the best of times."

"So he's just going to get away with it?"

Yuen rose. "It happens. Now I'm really sorry …"

I got up, grabbed my suitcase, and left. Neither of us said goodbye.

***

I stood on the steps of the police station, blinking in the sun and feeling a profound sense of displacement. For a brief, disquieting moment, I wondered if Yuen could be right, that I had misinterpreted perfectly ordinary events in my environment as threats. Yet the murder of Nick Duvall was real. Melnikov was real. The men in the truck were real. The shredded paintings were real. The explanation I had come up with fit all the facts. But it was clear that there would be no help forthcoming from the police.

I had arranged to spend the rest of the day with Melanie and her boys before returning to South Salish in the morning. I flagged down a passing taxi and sank into the back seat, hollow with fatigue and disillusionment.

Melanie eyed me sharply when she opened her door but waited until the clamour that had greeted my arrival died down and she had poured me a cup of coffee before asking what was wrong.

"Nothing." I had not told my family about any of the Nick Duvall business or the threats.

"You look terrible."

"Thanks."

"No, I mean it. Like you haven't slept in ages or something. Are you okay?"

I felt a sudden urge to unload but stopped; the last thing I wanted was to draw Melanie and her family into my nightmare. I nodded and smiled wanly. "I just got back from Europe—Italy. Still a bit jet-lagged."

"Wow. Aren't we the jetsetter now! Holiday? I wish I had known, I could have told you about some killer places to shop."

"It was just a short trip"—I paused—"to see some of Leo's family."

"Oh." Melanie lost interest, and we moved on to talk of our parents and my father's impending retirement.

***

The next morning, Kate was waiting for me at the dock in the little village on South Salish where the float plane landed. I held on to her an extra moment when she greeted me with a hug.

"Hey," Kate stepped back but held on to my arms. She studied my face. "You okay, hon?"

I shook my head.

Kate grabbed the handle of my suitcase. "Let's get you home."

Back at Southern Comfort, Hugh was eager to hear about my trip. "Sounds like it was pretty rough," Kate said.

"Not rough, exactly," I said, "but I think that I finally know what's going on."

Hugh raised his eyebrows. "Oh …?" he said.

"Look, do you mind if I wait to tell you? I think that Jean-Marie should hear about it too. He was in the line of fire as well, and there may be other ways in which he's affected."

I was thinking about the origins of my inheritance and whether I had the right to keep it. And without it, I didn't think I could afford the vineyard and winery. I had already drawn heavily on the line of credit Karen had set up for the expenditures to date, and a lot of money was still needed for construction, plant material, equipment, and, in the coming years, wages and operating expenses before there would be anything to sell.

Hugh glanced out the window in the direction of my place. "I saw them out there earlier today."

I made a move to go out and head over to the farm, but Kate stopped me. "Best I go. Jean-Marie said that there were some guys snooping around earlier this week."

***

Jean-Marie insisted on going home to change when Kate invited him to come over to hear my news. He and Dak had been digging drainage ditches, and both were caked with mud from the soppy soil.

Jean-Marie returned two hours later accompanied by Jasmine. When I greeted them, she raised her chin and said that she wanted to know about anything that might affect Jean-Marie. Dak had assumed that he was included in the invitation Kate had conveyed and also showed up at the appointed time, still damp from washing and trailing a whiff of smoke and resin.

When we all sat down at Kate's big table, I took the chair next to Jean-Marie. "Kate said some men had come to the farm."

Jean-Marie nodded.

"Did they say who they were or where they were from?"

"No, just that the farm was interesting and they thought to stop and ask what we were doing."

"What did they look like?"

"One, he had brown hair. The other one had no hair and was very big. They both wore the sunglasses, so I did not see their faces too good."

"Did they have accents at all?"

"Only one talked, the other, the one with no hair, just looked around. But the one who talked, he did not have any accent." Jean-Marie paused to accept a cup of coffee. "They asked who was the owner of the farm."

My heart thudded in my chest. "What did you say?"

Jean-Marie's lips twitched. "I hope it is okay; I said the vineyard was mine."

When the chatter died down and everyone turned to me expectantly, I hesitated before speaking. What was I doing involving these people in the mess I was in? I thought of Jean-Marie talking to those men. Were they just curious passersby, or were they the next wave, out to finish Melnikov's job? I thought of Dak fearlessly striding up to the cabin the morning after Melnikov had been there. His stick would be hardly enough if these guys came back. And then there were Kate and wheelchair-bound Hugh. It was just a matter of time before whoever was after me realized where I was staying. Kate wouldn't hesitate to take them on with her rifle, especially if Hugh was threatened; that was the problem.

After a few moments, Kate said, "You okay, hon?"

"I don't know," I said. "I'm wondering if it's right to burden you all with this information. It's put me in danger, and you may be better off not knowing it."

"Don't worry about it, hon. We're your friends; we want to help," Kate said. The others murmured their agreement.

I hesitated another moment, then nodded my head and re-told the account of that fateful night in Chibougamau as Signora Vitale knew it. "So I think that Robert Fournier was behind Nick Duvall's death, and that he then put out a contract on me, probably because he thought I was linked to Duvall," I said in conclusion.

"But why didn't he do something about Nick Duvall before this?" Jasmine said.

I shrugged. "I don't know. Maybe Fournier had forgotten about Nick Duvall all those years he was in prison." I turned to Jean-Marie. "Remember that old fellow in the bar?"

Jean-Marie nodded. "Gilles."

"He said he had seen Nick Duvall back in Chibougamau not long before we were there. Duvall was probably threatening to make trouble for Robert Fournier, much like he did with Leo."

"You should tell the police so they can get these guys off your back," Hugh said.

I smiled bleakly at him. "Your confidence in our law enforcement does you credit. I tried. Inspector Yuen doesn't believe me; he thinks I have an overactive imagination. And even if he did, he says that one, there's no hard evidence; two, it's too long ago; three, it's out of his jurisdiction; and four, he wouldn't want to take on a powerful politician." I had been counting the points off on my fingers and now linked them together, perhaps appropriately, as though in prayer.

"So what are you going to do now?" Kate said.

I sighed and shook my head. "I have absolutely no idea."

We sat in silence for several moments. Jasmine made an impatient gesture with her hand. "This is crazy. Why don't you just go to this Fournier guy and tell him to stop bugging you?"

Jean-Marie rested his hand on hers and said, "*Vraiment,* Jasmine."

"No, wait," I said slowly. "I have an idea."

Chapter 16

"Yes, I know I drink too much," Luc Brossard said.

I had declined his invitation to share the wine, and he had caught my glance as he refilled his glass from the carafe he had ordered.

I lifted a hand, palm out. "It's not my concern."

Luc took a sip and patted his mouth with his napkin. "No, I don't imagine that you have come all this way to discuss my appetite for alcohol."

We were having lunch in one of the dining rooms at Dorval airport. Planes slid in and out of view through the smoky plate glass window next to which we sat as they drew up to or away from their gates. Voices, and the sounds of heels and wheels tracking on industrial linoleum through long cavernous corridors, and of dishes and cutlery clinking merged into a screen of sound periodically pierced by announcements of arrivals and departures.

"The flight and hotel were okay?" I said.

"Oh, yes, perfectly fine." Luc chuckled. "The only problem was explaining to my wife that I was going to meet a woman. I told her not to worry; I am too old for mischief," he said. The gleam in his eyes made me wonder.

After my roundtable with Kate and Hugh and the others, I had found Luc Brossard's number on the Internet and called him with an invitation to meet me at Dorval at my expense. I said that I wanted to follow up on the conversation we had had in Chibougamau. Luc accepted my invitation, and although his voice revealed his sharpened interest, he asked only about the time, place, and travel arrangements. We agreed to meet in two days, and, yet again, I boarded an airplane.

Sitting across from Luc Brossard, I felt a sudden anxiety. When I had first met him, I sensed he was genuine, that he was being straight with us. What if my instincts were wrong? What if Luc Brossard was part of whatever collection of interests had gotten excited about the questions I had been asking in Chibougamau? It would explain how quickly they got on to me. Then I remembered Luc's regard for his friend Gilles, how he had slid the fifty-dollar bill I had left for the drinks to the old man. Yes, I was taking a chance, but it was a calculated one, and at this stage I had little choice.

"Ah, here's the food," I said. I hadn't wanted to start talking until we were settled and unlikely to be disturbed. The server tabled the plates and offered freshly ground pepper. When he and his foot-long grinder had departed, I began to speak.

"You know the robbery and murder of the man Didier that you spoke about?"

Luc stopped in the middle of raising his glass to his mouth and looked at me, his forehead wrinkled with perplexity. "What about it?"

"Did you ever catch whoever did it?"

Luc put his glass back down without drinking. "No, we didn't. But why do you ask?"

"I know what happened."

"*C'est pas vrai.*" Luc looked genuinely shocked. "How could you know?"

I put my fork down. My stomach wasn't ready for Cobb salad. "Let me get some coffee, then I'll tell you." I signalled for the server and raised my cup. "Could you just leave it please?" I said when he arrived. The server hesitated but set the pot on the table and left. Luc studied me with steely eyes, ignoring his food.

I swallowed some of the hot coffee and gave Luc Signora Vitale's account of what had happened the night Mario was fatally injured.

Luc uttered a string of profanities in French. He pushed his glass of wine aside, grabbed the coffee carafe, filled his cup, and stirred in two spoons of sugar. "So the commotion at the gas station was a decoy, a distraction. Yeah, it gave those guys an alibi, all right. I never would have linked them to the Didier business." He shook his head. "The bastards."

"The money that was taken was never returned, was it?"

"No."

"By the way, how much did they get?" I tried to keep my tone casual.

"Ooof," Luc said, his forehead creased with the effort of remembering. "Twelve, maybe thirteen thousand dollars, I think."

"Twelve thousand dollars! Is that all?"

"Well," Luc said, "it was a lot for that time."

"Apparently, at the jail, when Mario and Robert were about to be taken home, Nick gave Mario his share of the money so you police wouldn't find it on him. The idea was that Nick would get it back when he got out of jail. But that didn't happen until last year. That's probably why he was after Leo, and when he came to Chibougamau it was to see what he could shake out of Fournier."

Luc's eyes sparked with intelligence. "And that's probably what got him killed."

"But Fournier could have just paid him off."

"Who knows, maybe he did." Luc's face hardened. "Nick wouldn't have been killed because of blackmail; it would have been because of what he knew. Fournier has a lot to lose. A lot. The golden boy from Chibougamau. They say he is being courted for federal politics, maybe even for the top job. He couldn't afford to have a loose cannon like Duvall around, not with his ambitions."

Luc played with his thoughts for a moment then looked at me curiously. "But why are you concerning yourself with all this?"

I gazed off to the side for a moment then turned back to Luc. "I was with Nick Duvall when he was killed."

Luc sucked in his breath. "Ooof. That must have been tricky."

I nodded. "I think I was the top suspect for a while. Then a man started to follow me in Vancouver, someone the police said was with the Russian mafia. A contract killer, I figure, although I didn't know this at the time. He followed me home and scared the heck out of me. I had no idea why. I moved to another place I have, on an island. He found me there, came late at night. I heard him and got away just in time, but it was dark and he didn't know the terrain and fell off a cliff."

Luc's eyebrows shot up. "Now that would have been interesting to explain."

"Oh, it was. Fortunately the marks on the ground around where it happened showed that there was no one else with him when he went over. Then I found out that Nick Duvall and Leo were both from Chibougamau, and that's why I came out, to see if there was something that would explain what was going on and why someone was after me. But when I was in Chibougamau, my hotel room was ripped apart and my notebook, the one in which I was writing when I met with you, was taken. When we left town the next morning, we were followed by a couple of guys in a big truck. They had a gun, a rifle from the looks of it. They took a shot at us and tried to run us off the road."

Luc swore again. "Obviously they didn't."

I shook my head. "No, actually they were the ones who hit the ditch, rolled a few times."

Luc barked a laugh. "I remember hearing about that accident. So you drove them off instead."

"I didn't say that."

"Okay," Luc said, amused.

"What I still don't understand is how Fournier would have found out that I was in Chibougamau."

Luc topped up his coffee. He seemed to have forgotten about the wine. "Oh, it would have been the young guy in the bar. Fournier has a constituency office in Chibougamau and lots of staffers"—Luc made air quotes with his fingers—"hanging around. The kid is gone now."

"After I returned home from Quebec, someone broke into my place in Vancouver and slashed"—I cut a large X in the air—"a bunch of things, paintings, and furniture."

Luc's eyes widened. "You were there?"

"No, not at the time. I've been staying with friends. This last month has been hell. I can't live like this, always looking over my shoulder, watching my back. At the start, they were probably after me because they thought I knew about Fournier's involvement in the Didier death from Nick Duvall. Now that I do in fact know, well, I'm not sure that my position has worsened but I fully understand how bad it is. And it's probably just a matter of time before they figure out where I've been hiding."

"But you should tell the police, whoever is looking into Duvall's murder."

"Ha! I have, but he's closed the file on Nick Duvall's murder, says the Russian mafia guy who was after me did it, and he doesn't buy my theory that Fournier's behind everything because of what he and the others did to the old man in Chibougamau all those years ago. Even if he did, he says he can't do anything about it. Apart from the matter of jurisdiction, he says there's no real evidence, only hearsay."

Luc's forehead wrinkled in thought, and after a few moments he sighed and said, "He's right about that. It was clearly a robbery gone bad, but whatever evidence may have existed had been snowed over and the night deposit bag had only the old man's fingerprints. We asked around to see if anyone was splashing money about, buying new trucks they couldn't afford, that sort of thing, but nothing came up. We never would have guessed who was involved. Never." He poured himself more coffee and stirred it. "And even if Mario's mother comes forward—and it's unlikely she will, I think, because it would mean admitting her son's involvement—but if she does, it would still be, what, second-, third-hand. Hearsay. And after all this time. And against such a man."

"But wouldn't Mr. Didier's family want to see some justice after all these years?"

"The only family he had was an older sister. She never married either, and they lived together; in fact, there were some funny stories going around about them. But she died a couple of years before him. Didier was an old miser, tight-fisted, probably didn't like the idea of anyone getting his money. Anyhow, he never made a will. In the end, the store was sold and all the proceeds from that and the rest of his estate went to the government." Luc shook his head. "No, there's no one who would care."

We chewed on this for a few moments in silence. "I have an idea on how to stop this all," I said tentatively, "but I need your help, if you're willing."

Luc studied me with narrowed eyes and a faint smile. "I would be willing, yes, if it makes sense."

I leaned forward, lowered my voice. "Here is what I would like you to do."

Chapter 17

"Clare, it's a crazy idea," Hugh said.

I leaned across the table and patted his hand. "Dear, cautious, Hugh."

"No, I mean it." He glanced at the others sitting at the table, Kate, Jean-Marie, and Dak. "Talk about going into the lion's den."

"I'm hoping it's more like belling the cat," I said.

It was the next morning. I had just arrived on the floatplane from Vancouver and was bringing everyone up to date on my meeting with Luc Brossard.

I got up and paced around Kate and Hugh's kitchen. Having set what I hoped was the endgame in motion, I was jumpy with energy.

Jean-Marie cleared his throat. "Jasmine, she was just joking. She did not mean that you should do this."

I sat down again. "No, it was a good thought. Time to confront the matter. I can't hide anymore."

"But, Clare, hon, what will you do when you actually meet him? What will you say?" Kate said.

I picked apart the half-eaten muffin in my plate. "I'm not sure yet. Luc and I will work it out. The main thing right now is to get a meeting with Fournier. That's what Luc is working on."

Luc had said that Fournier was a busy man and it would take some time to set up. The wait was already intolerable. I pushed the plate of muffin crumbs away, slid down in my chair, and knotted my fingers together.

"This is a very dangerous move," Hugh said. "Clare, this guy wants you dead."

I unthreaded my fingers and straightened up. "What's the alternative? Running away? Getting a new identity?"

They all studied me, their faces stiff with concern. Even Dak had forgotten about his second muffin.

"Luc will be there; nothing will happen," I said.

"But what about after?" Hugh said. "This Fournier guy won't be very happy when you confront him. You've seen what he can do, how far his reach extends."

I shrugged and opened out my hands. "Well, then I guess I'll run away and change my identity." I said it lightly, but it was more than a possibility. "I just know that I can't live the way I have for these past few weeks."

"I will go with you to Fournier," Jean-Marie said.

I turned to him. "That's kind, but ..."

"No, I will come to—how do you say it?—watch your back."

Dak drew himself up. "I will come, too."

Kate leaned forward and put her hand over mine. "Clare, hon, Hugh and I would come too, if we could."

***

Jasmine insisted on accompanying Jean-Marie, so there were in fact four of us waiting for Luc Brossard in the anteroom to the chambers of the minister of finance in the legislative buildings of the Province of Quebec. Against Jean-Marie's protests, I had paid for everyone's flights and accommodation, milking the seemingly bottomless line of credit Karen had set up for the development of the vineyard. Still unaccustomed to my new financial status, I had to stop myself from calling her up to justify the withdrawals.

We made quite a group on the flight over. Heads turned as Jasmine sashayed down the aisle to her seat, resplendent in a multi-coloured jacket of some ethnic provenance, her luxurious hair floating around her. Dak followed, grinning from ear to ear at what turned out to be his first airplane ride. He was surprisingly well turned out in a greenish-brown tweed jacket, but the garment had obviously been kept in his hut and noses twitched as he walked by. Jean-Marie and I filed through last, slowly and sombrely; this was not a holiday.

When Luc arrived he shook my hand and, looking at the others with raised eyebrows, said, "When you told me to set up a meeting for *us,* I had assumed you meant you and me."

"These are my friends," I said firmly, and introduced them.

Luc, I observed, had dressed up for the occasion. The dark suit and crisp white shirt sharpened his natural authority. The contrast presented by his tie, a silk confection in rich jewel tones, served to heighten it even more. Luc caught me studying it. "My wife picks my ties," he said.

"I'd like to meet her sometime," I said, "if we come out of this intact." I was only half joking.

Luc smiled, but his eyes were serious. "If we don't, we won't be the only ones."

There was a commotion at the door to Fournier's office, and three men in business suits emerged. The goodbyes took a few minutes, then a man I assumed was Fournier conferred briefly with a young women who scribbled on a pad of paper while he talked. With a nod she took her leave, and Fournier turned to his secretary. She motioned towards us, and Fournier glanced in our direction, arranged his face into a welcoming expression, came towards us with his hand outstretched, and greeted Luc in French. Luc stepped forward and shook Fournier's hand. Jean-Marie, Jasmine, Dak, and I crowded behind him. Luc turned and introduced us. Fournier greeted Dak and Jean-Marie and made a little fuss over Jasmine, who stepped back a fraction of a step when he held on to her fingers a moment too long. Then the man who wanted me dead turned his pale blue-grey eyes on me and offered his hand. I had no choice but to take it.

I lost the next couple of minutes to fighting an impulse to flee. When I regained focus, we were inside Fournier's office and he was waving us to a small conference table that sat at one end. We all moved forward and arranged ourselves around the table. I took a seat as far away from Fournier as I could get.

I suddenly felt flattened by a profound lethargy, as though the ball of energy that had borne me through the two and a half weeks it had taken to set up the meeting had deflated. I ran my fingers along the marquetry that trimmed the edge of the table, tracing the vaguely Grecian fret pattern of pale inlaid wood. People were speaking, and, with effort, I raised my head and forced myself to listen.

Luc and Robert Fournier exchanged small talk in English about events in Chibougamau and Luc's retirement. I studied Fournier: He was of average height and build and had the soigné appearance that spoke of expensive hairstylists, manicures, and massages. A slight roll under his chin hinted at a soft body under the impeccably cut grey suit. A deep tan that was just starting to fade pointed to a recent tropical vacation and set off his curiously pallid eyes and fair hair to good effect. I searched his face; nowhere was there any sign that he was a killer.

I tuned in when Fournier got down to business. "So, Luc, what's brought you all here?" Fournier included the rest of us with a gracious gesture.

"I would like to thank you for agreeing to see us, Minister," Luc said. Fournier's head dipped slightly in acknowledgement of Luc's formality. "I know that you are a very busy man, and we won't take up much of your time. But I wanted you to meet Clare Tamm." Luc gestured down the table, and Fournier gave me a neutral glance.

He has no idea who I am, I thought. *He has had people follow me and threaten me and destroy my property, and he doesn't even know to whom he is doing it.*

"I haven't known Clare long," Luc continued, "but she has become a good friend. And I am very concerned about some of the things that have been happening to her recently. People have been breaking into her home and threatening her."

Fournier received this information with what appeared to be genuine puzzlement. "I am not sure how I can help," he said, turning up his palm. I felt a stab of uncertainty. Could we be wrong? Were we possibly completely off base in thinking that this man was behind it all?

"Well, you see, some of this happened near Chibougamau," Luc said. "Clare was visiting there a few weeks ago with Jean-Marie." Luc nodded in Jean-Marie's direction. Fournier's eyes flicked around the table, from Jean-Marie to me, then to Jasmine, no doubt wondering why a man with a wife like Jasmine would be tootling around with a woman like me. Luc continued, "Someone chased them on the road, two men in a truck. And they shot at Clare and Jean-Marie as well. Fortunately, the men drove their truck off the road before they did any serious harm."

Fournier glanced at me again with the glimmering of awareness in his eyes. He turned back to Luc. "Still, I don't know what I can do."

"You are a man of considerable influence," Luc said, "and you have many resources. Perhaps you could have someone inquire about who might have been behind this and maybe get them to stop."

Fournier straightened in his chair. He finally knew what we were doing there. "I have resources, yes, but I am obliged to use them in a way that concerns my office and my constituency." He glanced at me. "Mademoiselle, ah ..."

"Tamm," Luc said.

"Yes, Mademoiselle Tamm and Monsieur ... Lebeau, was it?" Jean-Marie nodded. "You say they were visitors to Chibougamau. While I am very sorry that they had such an unpleasant experience, perhaps it was something personal, perhaps they brought the trouble with them and these men were not even from Chibougamau. Besides, neither of them are constituents, so I don't see why it would be my concern."

Luc leaned back in his chair, propped his elbows on the armrests, and steepled his fingers. "Clare was engaged to Leo Barsoni. Leo died last winter, and the reason Clare came to Chibougamau was to, you know, see where Leo came from, visit his childhood home and so on.

"You knew the Barsonis back then, didn't you? You and Mario Barsoni were good friends, I think," Luc continued. "Such a tragedy that Mario died, and so young. You were with him when he was injured, weren't you?"

"That was a very long time ago," Fournier said, his lips barely moving.

"It was, but, you know, I still remember that night well because of all the things that happened." Luc sat up and settled himself more comfortably in his chair. "Anyhow, Mario's death and all that stuff inevitably came up when Clare was talking to people in Chibougamau. Lots of memories that were long buried got stirred up, and we're thinking maybe this has got someone upset."

"Luc, all this ancient history." Fournier's face cracked in a tight smile. "It is always nice to reminisce, but"—he gestured around his office—"this is perhaps not the time or the place." He looked at his watch and started to rise. "Now, I regret very much, I am expected at a committee meeting."

We've accomplished nothing, I realized with a shock. Luc had said that he'd lead the exchange with Fournier, but he has been too oblique, thrusting with these vague barbs, and Fournier's just dancing out of the way. Now he's throwing us out, and nothing's been resolved. My ears started to buzz, my mind to effervesce. I slowly rose out of my chair and leaned over the table, propping myself up on my fingertips. "Sit down," I said.

Fournier turned to look at me as though surprised that I was still there.

"We know what you did. We know about Didier, the robbery and the murder," I said.

Fournier froze. The others turned startled faces toward me.

"We know about Nick Duvall."

"What do you know about Nick Duvall?" Fournier's voice was smooth, expressionless. I noted that he didn't ask who Nick Duvall was.

"You forgot about him, didn't you, locked away for so long? But then he shows up, reminds you of the Didier business, probably asks for some money to be quiet. You realized that you'd never be rid of him and you had to do something."

"*Putain!*" Fournier said through clenched teeth. It must have meant something pretty bad, because Jean-Marie rose, Dak following him a half-second later. Jasmine grasped Jean-Marie's sleeve and looked at him with alarm. Luc slowly shook his head. I ignored him.

"And I can only assume that you wanted me dead because you figured I was somehow part of Duvall's deal, that I knew what he knew, that I also would come after you. The funny thing is that I didn't, not for a long time, but now I do, and so does everyone else in this room. These are my witnesses."

It struck me that my witnesses may well have been regretting their offers to accompany me, wondering what I had got them into. I wasn't sure myself. *Don't start something you don't know how to finish,* my boss Simon had once said after an unsatisfactory exchange with a client. Well, I had done just that.

No one spoke; everyone remained motionless in their places. Fournier still crouched halfway out of his chair, poised, a cobra ready to strike. He held my gaze with those eyes that were the colour of frozen water. *Yes,* I thought, *you could kill someone and not turn a hair.*

174

Fournier broke the silence. "You have no proof."

"No we don't," I said, "*and that's the whole point.*" I pulled back, stood tall, glad for perhaps the first time of my superior height. "So stop it, get those goons off my back, and leave me the *hell* alone." My voice had been rising as I spoke, and the last few words came out in a roar.

Fournier slowly straightened up. He glanced around the table, then back at me. "If I hear anything, if anyone so much as breathes a word, makes even the smallest suggestion that I had anything to do with any of this, I will come down on you so hard, I will—"

I cut him off. "And *I* have made arrangements for all of this to be disclosed should anything violent and unexplained happen to me or to any of these people here." I hadn't, actually, having just thought of it, but would file something with Karen as soon as I got back to Vancouver. If I got back: I had a vision of Fournier somehow arranging to blow up our airplane. The room suddenly felt too small, the air too thick; I couldn't share either a second longer with Fournier. I jerked my head in the direction of the door and said to the others, "Let's get out of here."

***

I walked out, strode down the long corridor to the ornate rotunda of the legislative building, and marched through the front door and down the long run of steps, not stopping until I was well away. The others caught up to me after a few seconds and closed around me in a circle. No one spoke. They were, I think, dumfounded.

"Do you think it will work?" Jasmine finally said. Did I detect a grain of respect in her voice?

I drew in a deep breath. "You know, I don't really care. If they still come after me, if that's my fate, well, I guess that's that."

Luc put a hand on my shoulder. "You were *magnifique*, eh?"

I didn't feel magnificent. My shoulders sagged, my legs were jelly, I was unspeakably weary. "Let's go home," I said.

Chapter 18

Home. Ah, now where would that be?

When we returned to Vancouver, I parted company with Jean-Marie, Jasmine, and Dak at the arrivals hall of the airport. They headed to the departure gate for the plane to Victoria, from where they would catch the ferry back to South Salish; I caught a taxi to a hotel. It was time, I thought, to resume the life that Leo's death and all that had followed had so rudely interrupted.

I stayed in the hotel for the three weeks it took to arrange for a moving company to empty Leo's condo and for me to repaint and refurnish it. I wanted no reminders.

I admit to looking over my shoulder for the first few days, starting if someone moved abruptly, scanning crowds for men who looked like gangsters. Eventually I relaxed my vigilance, but I never completely lost a heightened sense of my surroundings.

The probate for Leo's will finally concluded. My meeting with Karen to deal with all the paperwork was scheduled for late morning, and when we were done her secretary brought in a selection of tiny sandwiches, two flute glasses, and a half bottle of Veuve Clicquot and set them down on Karen's small boardroom table. We moved from

Karen's desk to the table, and Karen picked up the bottle of champagne, tore off the foil, loosened the little wire cage, and wiggled the cork free. The wine frothed up and over the side of the first glass she filled. "Wooo!" she said, hurriedly setting the glass down on a paper napkin. She poured the second glass out more carefully and held it out to me.

"Congratulations, Clare. It's not every day that someone becomes a millionaire."

I accepted the glass and sat down. "If it's really mine."

"What?" Karen slowly lowered herself into her chair.

The champagne went flat and the bread on the sandwiches curled while I told Karen what I had learned about Leo's past and the fateful night in Chibougamau. "I think this was the source of the money for Leo's properties and investments and why he kept them apart and secret."

"But it was only, what? Six, seven thousand dollars? And the portfolio's worth eight million plus," Karen said.

"Yes, he must have invested it very shrewdly." I had casually asked my brother-in-law Dave, a financial wizard, whether six thousand dollars invested in the early seventies could have been made to grow to eight million dollars over twenty-five years, and if so, how.

"Oh, yeah, if you started some kind of business," Dave had said.

"Let's say it wasn't through a business."

"Then real estate," Dave had said. "It would have been more than enough for a down payment then. You start with one property and then use it to leverage the purchase of others. You know, like the fairy tale about the cobbler who first made one pair of shoes, and with the proceeds had the means to make two pairs, and so on and so on? Property's worth a lot more now in real terms compared to twenty-five years ago.

"And then, of course, there are stocks: high-tech, energy, gold. Oh, yeah, if you had had a bit of seed money, took some risks, and were lucky, you could have done well over that time."

"All the property Leo had," I said to Karen, "if he had purchased it early on, it would be worth a lot now."

"You know, Leo did own the house he lived in while we were going to university. He had renters as well, upstairs and in a basement suite. I had assumed that, with his parents dead, he had inherited some money."

"I got the sense that Leo's family didn't have much to begin with, and I doubt Leo's stepmother was very generous when she disowned him."

"I suppose so." Karen sighed. "But with Nick Duvall, why didn't Leo just pay him off? It cost him his life."

"I've wondered about that as well. Maybe Leo did but Nick wanted more and was threatening him with exposure. After all, the money he kept had been stolen."

Karen looked at me, bewildered. "So where does it leave us?"

"It leaves me with a problem. There's a very good chance Leo's wealth was built on the proceeds of a crime. I'm not comfortable with that."

Karen opened out her hands in exasperation. "But what can we do about it now? Didn't you say that the fellow who was robbed had no descendants?"

"He didn't, no." I leaned forward. "I thought I would set up a charitable fund."

Karen choked on the sip of wine she had just taken. She grabbed a handful of tissues from the box on her desk and pressed them against her mouth. "You're going to give all that money away?"

I shook my finger. "No, not all of it. I've calculated what six thousand dollars would be worth today if invested in, say, government savings bonds. Interest rates then were about 7.5 percent, but they fluctuated quite a bit over the twenty-five years, and there also is inflation to consider."

Karen's forehead wrinkled. "You've lost me, Clare."

I waved the details away. "Anyhow, six thousand dollars invested conservatively in 1973 with compounding interest would be worth around seventy thousand dollars now."

"But that's much less than the value of Leo's estate."

"Yes, I know. So the bulk of it, the millions, were due to his own efforts."

"Does that make you feel better about the whole thing now?"

"To some degree. But I'd still like to make some form of restitution."

"But what kind? And to whom?"

"Let's say that the original six thousand dollars was a loan to Leo, albeit one of dubious origin. On his behalf, I'd like to make a contribution to society that is an apology for the crimes that were committed to get the money and a thank you for its use all these years. I thought I'd put a million dollars into a trust to fund some appropriate good works."

"Isn't that a bit excessive, Clare?"

"Maybe," I said, "but you can't do much with anything less. What I had in mind was creating a scholarship based in Quebec for teens who are at risk of going astray. Someone like Mario was all those years ago. It would be for training—of any kind, it doesn't have to be university—that gives them a chance to make something of themselves and their lives that they might not otherwise get. I'm going to ask Luc Brossard to administer this fund. He'll know how to find these kids, and I trust him absolutely to look after the money.

"Doing this would make me feel a whole lot better about keeping the rest of the money, which I consider to be Leo's, earned through his ingenuity and enterprise."

Karen studied me without saying anything.

"What do you think?" I said. It had made sense before, but now I wondered if this solution to my moral dilemma was a bit too convenient.

Karen cocked an eyebrow. "I think it's very Jesuitical."

***

Over the next few weeks I was engrossed in the surreal task of tending to my millions. I informed myself completely about each of the investments, picking through the financials of the properties, tracking the performance of each of the securities. It was during this time that the human resources department of my old firm contacted me. Since the accident I had been on sick leave, and they wanted to know if and when I planned to return. The call flustered me; I had completely forgotten about work. *Should I return?* I wondered. Well, why not? My new-found assets seemed to be managed reasonably well and didn't need my interference, so what else was I going to do?

I arranged to meet the head of my old division, not Simon, who, I learned from Adrienne, had been assigned to head a project in Malaysia, but a woman in her early forties named Emily. Emily's mouse-brown hair was cut in a short sensible style, and she wore a severe navy linen suit and low-cut cream blouse. Her manner was bristly, her tone suspicious. She said that, it being summer, there was no immediate billable work for me. She didn't have to point out that this would make me a drain on her budget and mess up her performance measures. I said it was no problem; I could wait until the fall, traditionally a season when new projects came on stream, to return.

While preoccupied with my new obligations, I hadn't thought much about South Salish, the farm, and my friends there, just exchanging the occasional email with Kate and Hugh. Then Jean-Marie called one day. When we had decided to proceed with the vineyard, I had diverted some of the money from the line of credit to an account at a bank on the island on which Jean-Marie could draw for day-to-day expenditures. The money was almost all gone now, he said, and there also were some large payments to be made, especially for the construction of the pump house.

"The what?" I said.

"It is for the water and the irrigation."

"I had better come out."

"Yes, that would be good," Jean-Marie said.

***

"Clare, hon, I'm so sorry, but we're totally booked up. Summer, you know. And Elliot's here for all of July," Kate said when I called to let her know I was coming. I said it was okay, I would stay in the cabin, but the idea didn't enthrall me. Left vacant all this time, it would probably need a good cleaning, and after the business with Valerian Melnikov, I wasn't sure how I would feel living there.

The early evening ferry I took to South Salish had to return to the terminal because of a medical emergency, and what with the complicated process of removing the ill man to the ambulance, then unloading and reloading the cars to let the man's wife drive their vehicle off, I did not arrive on the island until after midnight. Heavy clouds obscured the moon and stars, and as I drove up to the cabin I had to hunch over the steering wheel to see the tracks on the overgrown driveway. As I approached the cabin, I realized that I did not have the key, nor did I remember returning it to the hiding place on the ledge when I had fled, eons ago, it seemed, over the fence to Kate and Hugh's. It turned out not to matter; the door was unlocked.

The cabin was as I had left it, the book I had flung away still on the corner of the sofa where it had landed, the cups from the coffee I had had with Dak still in the drain tray. A fine layer of dust coated every surface.

***

I slept late, and on rising wandered down the driveway to see Jean-Marie and Dak. At the turn where the farm's fields came into full view, I stopped abruptly. A forest of posts had sprouted on the gentle slopes, and a cluster of vehicles surrounded the skeleton of a building at the edge of what had been the pond and was now a miniature lake.

I was gripped by a sense of outrage, the same as I had felt when my family had left me at home with a friend of my mother's and carried on with a long-planned and paid-for trip to Disneyland after I had been stricken with measles. I tracked Jean-Marie down with long, angry strides and, sweeping my arm in a grand arc, said without preamble, "What's going on here?"

Jean-Marie's welcoming smile morphed into an expression of astonishment. "*Mais,* we do what is necessary to be ready for the planting this fall."

"But I wasn't here."

Jean-Marie raised his shoulders, opened out his hands. "I did not know I should wait. You are not here, you did not say to wait."

I looked away, fighting tears. The sense of betrayal I felt was, I knew, quite irrational. "Look, we'll talk later. I want to say hello to Kate and Hugh," I said, trying to keep my voice steady, and headed off before I could say something I'd regret.

When I knocked on Kate and Hugh's door, it was opened quickly. "Clare!" said Kate. "Hugh's in the back." She closed the door behind me and hurried towards a pair of voices in the sitting room speaking over each other, the male soft and cultured, the female trenchant.

Hugh exclaimed with delight when he saw me. He took off his reading glasses and set them on the newspaper he had been reading. I dropped a kiss on his cheek and my bottom into a lawn chair by the table where he sat.

"Have they left yet?" Hugh said.

I shook my head. "Difficult?"

"Not really, at least he isn't. A bit absent-minded, though. They've been looking for their car keys since breakfast. But, never mind; how are you?"

I looked away at a bed dense with flowers, pink and coral gladiola spears rearing up at the back, a jumble of pastel-coloured snapdragons buzzing with bees along the front. "I'm not sure," I said.

"They're not still after you, are they?"

I lifted my eyes to Hugh's concerned gaze and shook my head. "No, I think that's well and truly over."

"What, then?"

Kate came outside and saved me from having to answer. I rose, and we hugged. "Sorry, Clare, but I had to deal with those two."

"Did they find the keys?" Hugh said.

Kate nodded. "In the sofa cushions, thank goodness. I was just about to call Al, the mechanic." She turned to me. "Anyhow, how the heck are you, hon? It's been ages."

"Something's up," Hugh said. "Clare was about to tell me."

In the brief interval created by Kate's arrival, I had come to realize how ridiculous my reaction was. So when I spoke, it was a bit sheepishly. "All the work that's been done at my place, the posts, and the work on that building, well, it's kind of upset me."

"Wasn't it done right?" Kate said.

I shook my head. "That's not it. I didn't know it was going on."

"Didn't Jean-Marie tell you what he was doing?" Hugh said.

I remembered the pages of hand-written plans Jean-Marie had given to me in the spring. "Well, yeah, but I'd forgotten and I've been a bit preoccupied with other stuff."

"But why's it a problem? He seems to know what he's doing."

"It's really stupid," I said, my cheeks burning, "but I'm feeling sort of left out."

Kate and Hugh glanced at each other and burst out laughing. "There's a simple remedy, hon," Kate said. "Get involved. After all, it is your place."

***

By way of apology to Jean-Marie, I asked him to take me through all he had done and his plans for what was to come. He told me the hay in the meadow had been mowed, then the fields plowed up to loosen the soil and break through the hardpan. As we walked through the rows of posts, he pointed out that they ran north-south, the optimal orientation for catching the sun's rays. He explained how the posts had been punched into the ground by a backhoe. In the middle of the field, Jean-Marie squatted down and scooped up some soil, explaining that the labs tests he had had done indicated that the soil was more acidic than was ideal for grapevines. "Tomorrow, we start to put down the dolomite lime to make the soil less acid."

"I'd like to help, if I can," I said.

Jean-Marie stood up and his brow cleared. "*Bien sûr.*"

After this, I presented myself every morning for work. Over the next couple of days, Jean-Marie, Dak, and I walked up and down the rows carrying pails of lime and broadcasting the granules by hand. During this time, a flatbed truck delivered several large spools of wire. Jean-Marie loaded these on a rotating spindle mounted on the back of the all-terrain vehicle, and while Dak and I took turns drawing down multiple lengths of wire to the end of each row, Jean-Marie guided the wire off the spindle and cut the length free when it was long enough. When the wire lengths had all been measured out and cut, Jean-Marie handed me a hammer and a carpenter's apron full of clips, and I helped him and Dak nail the clips into the posts at set intervals to place the wire strands at different heights to support the vines as they grew. The lowest wire was intended to support the irrigation hose, and this was the next task. Jean-Marie and Dak dug trenches from the pump house, which was nearing completion, to the heads of the rows and laid sections of white plumbing pipe along its length, connecting them with plumber's glue at the joins. Then we spooled out lengths of black irrigation hose with perforations to allow the water to slowly drip out onto the ground along each row, and while Jean-Marie connected the hose to the water pipes, Dak and I tied the irrigation hose to the lowest wire with zap straps.

I fell naturally into the peaceful natural rhythms of the physical work, and the time swiftly passed. My only connections to the outside world were communications with my family, Karen, and Luc Brossard, who had enthusiastically accepted the task of setting up the scholarship I had proposed. In one of his emails, Luc sent me a snippet from one of Montreal's English language dailies. It said that Robert

Fournier, Quebec's minister of finance, had resigned to accept an unspecified position with the Inter-Parliamentary Union in Geneva. Luc's take on the news was that the move was one of self-protection, that Fournier had worked his extensive network to find a hidey-hole far away from any threat posed by those of us who knew what he had done. A quick Internet search revealed that the Inter-Parliamentary Union was a longstanding and earnest body whose activities, while worthwhile, appeared to be excruciatingly tedious. There were, I supposed, different forms of punishment.

***

One morning I was lingering over a cup of coffee—Jean-Marie and Dak were doing something mechanical and didn't need my help—when the telephone rang.

"Clare, hi," said a male voice when I answered. The voice was familiar, but I couldn't immediately put a name to it.

"Yes?"

"It's Simon."

The image of my former boss formed in my mind. "Ah, yes, hello. I thought you were in Malaysia?"

"I am. I'm back here to report in. The brass are doing a major project review. Listen, I heard you're coming back next week."

I felt an odd sensation, like a light blow to the solar plexus. There was a calendar tucked under the local phone book, and I tugged it free. It was folded open at July, the picture a rainforest scene, the giant trees strung with moss. I flipped the page over to the next month where the image was a pair of orcas breaching against the backdrop of a misty fjord. I drew my finger down to the last week. Today was garbage day, so it was a Wednesday, and that meant that it was the twenty-ninth of August.

"I … yes, I guess I talked to Emily about it," I said.

"Look, before Emily gets you involved in something: I really could use you in Malaysia. The project's scope has expanded, and I need someone else, someone I can trust. It would be two years, Clare. A terrific opportunity, and Kuala Lumpur's a fantastic place. Great base for touring through the region. What do you think?"

I would have been flattered if I hadn't known Simon so well. He was a great talker, terrific dealing with clients, but a complete loss at doing the actual research and writing the reports. He was looking for a dogsbody to take care of business while he swanned around keeping everyone happy. But still. It *was* quite an opportunity. I sat down slowly at the table. "How soon would you need me?"

"As soon as you could get out there. I mean, you're footloose and fancy-free now, right? By the way, how're you feeling?"

My mind tried to wrap itself around Simon's proposal, and I didn't answer.

"Clare?"

"Yes, Simon, I'm still here. Look, I need to think about this."

"Clare, it's right up your alley. High-level stuff. Organizational planning and program development. Client's the minister of industry and science. You're not going to get another chance like this easily."

"Look, it's definitely appealing, but I just can't give you an answer right away."

"Well, don't take too long. I'm going back on the weekend, and I need to know by then."

"I understand." I noted Simon's telephone number and said I'd be back to him in a day or two.

***

Malaysia! Wow! My heart skipped around at the thought. Leo had been there once on business and said it was beautiful and a place he wanted to return to sometime. What an adventure it would be: different landscapes, new people, exotic food, an exciting project! But ... I looked around and a stone formed in my stomach. It would mean going away for a long time, if not for good, leaving behind my family, my new friends, abandoning the farm.

I sat for a long time, alternating between excitement and despondency. When I had wound myself into a state of total confusion, I rose, grabbed a pair of gloves and a hat, and wandered down to the fields.

The default job when anyone was at loose ends was to pick rocks. The work involved moving them from the alleys formed by the rows of posts to the space between them where the vines would grow. The idea was to clear the ground for mowing, as stone and pebbles dull a mower's blades and can be cast up like projectiles when it passes. Putting them under the vines had the further advantage of discouraging weeds from growing and competing with the vines for nutrients as well as collecting and reflecting heat up on the leaves and fruit.

I recommend rock-picking to anyone with a troubled heart. A mindless task, it allows your thoughts to follow their own course. The rhythm—pick up, put down—soothes. You move along bent over at the waist, the extra blood flowing to the head perhaps enriching the brain. The mass of the stones in the hand is reassuring, their textures, grainy, sharp, smooth, speak of endurance, of time itself. Most predate life as we know it. I was hefting a mottled blue-grey rock, vaguely trapezoidal in shape, polished by the waters of the prehistoric lake that Hugh said had once washed against the slopes of the farm, when Jean-Marie came up to me.

"I am going home now," Jean-Marie said.

I looked around. Was it late afternoon already?

"Dak, he is going to fish on the boat with his friend until next week."

"Okay," I said vacantly.

Jean-Marie nodded and turned to leave. I stretched out a hand as though to stop him. "Jean-Marie …"

Jean-Marie paused and turned back to me. My hand dropped. I wasn't sure what I was trying to do.

"Is there something?" Jean-Marie said.

A sudden surge of emotion closed my throat. I swallowed and said, "I've been offered a job, some very interesting work, but it is in Malaysia, and it would be for at least two years."

"Ah," Jean-Marie said. The lines of his face shifted into neutral. When he didn't say more, I asked him what he thought I should do. "It is not for me to say," he said.

"But you must have some reaction. I would like to know. If I went, you'd be left alone here to do things the way you want, without me bothering you. Maybe you'd prefer it that way?"

Jean-Marie's eyes dropped to the ground. He nudged a stone to the side with the toe of one of his shoes. I noticed that the leather was frayed on a spot and the metal cap of the toe showed through. "No," he said, raising his eyes to mine. "Not really. But if you want very much to do this job, then you should go."

I nodded. After a long moment, Jean-Marie said, "*À demain,*" and turned and walked away. I watched his retreating back until he reached his truck, climbed in, and drove off. Looking down, I realized that I was still holding the blue-grey rock. It nestled comfortably against the folds in my glove, as though at home in the palm of my hand.

"You silly twit," I said to the rock. "You don't need Simon."

Chapter 19

We planted the vineyard in early October, the week before Thanksgiving. Dak and I stood in respectful silence as Jean-Marie manoeuvred the forklift—the most recent addition to our stable of machines—to unload the pallets bearing the ten thousand vines. Jean-Marie assembled a planting crew of twenty-one people. Some were guys he knew in the landscaping business, the rest were from the community of travellers and itinerant folk who had washed up on the shores of South Salish Island. With this crew, Jean-Marie figured the work would be completed in four days.

Jean-Marie told the workers to be at the farm by eight thirty on the day we planned to start, and several were, but the remainder straggled in over the next half hour with excuses that included alarms not going off, not being able to get a ride, having to do a chore beforehand, getting off at the wrong farm, and, with questionable candour, being kept in bed by a demanding girlfriend. The workers milled about, making introductions and helping themselves to coffee from an urn Kate had set out on a table against the wall of the pump house.

Jean-Marie stood nearby waiting, with apparent passivity, for the last of the workers to arrive. I had come to recognize the controlled impatience in the rigid line of his back and clenched jaw. I snapped one of the little plant pots from the tray to which it had been attached and studied the spindly twig that grew out of a mix of moss and soil.

"It doesn't look like much," I said, turning it over in my hand. "Hard to imagine that this will eventually grow to be a big, thick vine."

Jean-Marie turned away from his scrutiny of the workers. He relaxed marginally and smiled. "Yes, I always think it is like a miracle." He glanced at his watch. "Okay, enough." He clapped his hands for attention and motioned the workers to step forward. He ran through the whole operation, identifying different tasks and telling individual workers the ones to which they had been assigned. Some would finish digging holes to receive the vines; some would distribute the trays of tiny plants along the rows and generally serve as runners. A couple of people would drop a small amount of bone meal in each hole in advance of the planters. Twelve people would be left to plant the vines, and Jean-Marie would demonstrate to these the correct way of doing so. As everyone dispersed to their tasks, Jean-Marie turned to me. "And what would you like to do, *Patronne?*" he said.

"Plant," I said. "I want to plant the vines."

***

In the end, it took seven days to complete the planting. It rained on the third day, and each morning the crew shrunk in size; some had commitments, and for others the work was too demanding. My parents, my father now retired and at loose ends, came out to observe the operation. I lodged them in my cabin and bunked down in one of Kate and Hugh's guest rooms. Hugh's son Elliot, a gangly, pimply fifteen-year-old, came out for the Thanksgiving weekend. For all his blushing and inarticulate mumbling, he worked hard and steadily, and often he and I were the last to come in at the end of the day.

Each morning, when I kneeled to plant the first vine, I entered a different world. I would snap a little pot from its tray and tip the plant and its plug of peat moss into my hand, then gently set it in the hole that had been dug, deep enough to cover the roots but not too deep. Then, taking care not to topple over, I would hold the plant in place with one hand while, with the other, I scooped the soil that had been left on the side back into the hole. I would finish by patting the soil down firmly around the plant to collapse any air pockets that could damage the fragile roots. Then on to the next hole, the next plant. I would either rise and crouch down again like a piston or, as the day wore on, shuffle from hole to hole on my knees. My back ached, my shoulders burned, my knees creaked, but I loved every moment: the taste of the wind, the bird calls, the dark, sweet smell of the earth crumbling between my fingers.

My memories of the time are a montage of images and impressions: workers swarming the field like ants; Jean-Marie coolly directing everyone; Dak walking back after digging the last hole, shovel on his shoulder, grinning ear to ear; Kate and my mother hysterical when one visiting dog started to hump another under one of the food tables; one of the itinerant workers, a painfully thin man in his thirties, stuffing cookies and bananas into the pockets of his tattered slicker; my father singing Estonian folk songs as he and Hugh unpacked the little plant pots. And above all, the satisfaction of seeing yet another vine planted, another hole filled.

On the afternoon of the seventh day, when it was all done, I walked with my father back from the last row that had been planted. In the end, we were down to a crew of only four, and he had tried to help out by dropping the bone meal in the holes in advance of the planters.

"You've done something good here, daughter," he said.

We stopped and turned to look back at the vineyard, as now it officially was. Row upon row of little twigs poked their heads out of the ground. I smiled wearily. "Who would have thought?"

"Yes," he said. "Your mother and I, we worried about you, the accident and then taking on this place and starting this vineyard. But it was inspired, I see that now. I envy you in a way, setting down roots, finding something to grow, to build." His voice trailed off.

I looked at him. The slanting late-afternoon light deepened the lines on his face. They were sad lines. "Are you missing teaching?" I said.

"No, not teaching, particularly. After a while it became simply a tape that looped round and round, and students seemed less and less enthusiastic." He fell silent, and I waited. We had never spoken like this before, as adults, as equals. "What it is, what I miss, is the sense of anticipation that comes with taking something on. I can't accept that there will never be anything more that I will do. I am not ready to go quietly into the night."

"Your life is far from over." I said carefully. I remembered the music that had filled our house when I was young, the radio, Dad's records, the ensembles with whom Dad had once played violin and guitar. He had stopped, he claimed, to concentrate on his job. "Why not play music again?"

Dad grimaced. "I have long known the limits of my talent. You know what they say: Those who can, do; those who can't, teach."

"Come on, Dad, we're not talking Carnegie Hall."

Dad glanced at me with a half-smile. "Maybe. But here ..." His gesture encompassed the field before us. "Look at you."

"Yes, and it proves that just about anything is possible, doesn't it?"

***

I thought of my dad and his music again a few nights later. I had hitched a ride with Kate and Hugh to an event at the hall that served as the venue for theatre and live entertainment on South Salish. The performers were an amateur troupe of flamenco dancers from Vancouver. They danced with more enthusiasm than skill, but the audience loved them for their charm and exuberance. No *duende* there; they all sported huge smiles. The crowd's favourite was a young woman of generous proportions who sported her ruffles with great élan and whose foot stomps reverberated through the room.

Afterward Kate offered to drive me right up to the cabin, but I said that I wanted to walk. It was a breathlessly beautiful night. I stopped on the driveway and looked out to the fields. The harvest moon was so full and ripe it sagged under the weight of its brilliance and oozed light onto the long, silent rows of tiny vines that sloped down the hill. I stood for a moment drinking in the scene, feeling at home and at peace. A frisson of pure joy ran through my body. The flamenco rhythms still echoed in my mind, and I lifted my arms, arched my back, and stamped my feet. It felt ridiculous and wonderful at the same time. One of Dad's favourite songs, "Moondance" by Van Morrison, popped into my head. When the song came on, he would sweep my mother into his arms and dance her around the room, crooning the words into her ear while Melanie and I giggled and groaned.

I stopped dancing, struck by a thought. *Now that it's a real vineyard, you've got to give it a name,* Kate had said, and more than once. Even Jean-Marie had raised the matter of naming the farm. *Yes, I should,* I had thought, *and before you do.* I actually had given the matter some consideration. Everything suggested that I should acknowledge Leo somehow in the name; it had been his idea, and his legacy was financing it. And yet, and yet. His life and his memory evoked such sorrow. For the lonely boy he had been, for the emotional scars he bore, for the life together we were denied. I hesitated to encumber the vineyard with such sadness. It was a place of possibilities, of the future, and it had a character, a presence even, in its own right. The name needed to reflect this spirit.

"I think ...," I said, addressing the land glazed with ethereal light that spread out before me, "I think I will call you Moondance."

Leo would have understood, I thought. I suddenly felt his absence acutely. Throughout the frantic weeks when I was uncovering the story of his life and unravelling the mystery of his legacy, he had been with me. Now there was only the night, and the moon, and Leo's gift—this land. I sighed and continued on my solitary way.

Acknowledgements

Thanks to Gail Bowen for helping me find Clare's voice, to Dinah Forbes for her encouragement and advice on plot and pacing, to Carolyn Swayze for her valuable comments, and to the team at Iguana Books for bringing *Root Causes* to life.

Iguana Books
iguanabooks.com

If you enjoyed *Root Causes*...
Look for other books coming soon from Iguana Books! Subscribe to our blog for updates as they happen.

iguanabooks.com/blog/

You can also learn more about Elaine Kozak and her upcoming work on her blog.

elainekozak.iguanabooks.com/blog/

If you're a writer ...
Iguana Books is always looking for great new writers, in every genre. We produce primarily ebooks but, as you can see, we do the occasional print book as well. Visit us at iguanabooks.com to see what Iguana Books has to offer both emerging and established authors.

iguanabooks.com/publishing-with-iguana/

If you're looking for another good book ...
All Iguana Books books are available on our website. We pride ourselves on making sure that every Iguana book is a great read.

iguanabooks.com/bookstore/

Visit our bookstore today and support your favourite author.

IGUANA

CPSIA information can be obtained at www.ICGtesting.com
Printed in the USA
LVOW08s0021080414

380691LV00002B/42/P